I0642736

HAUNTED WASTELANDS

HAUNTED WASTELANDS SERIES

BOOK 1

IAN FORTEY
AND
RON RIPLEY

EDITED BY ANNE LAO
AND DAWN KLEMISH

ISBN: 979-8-89476-290-6
Copyright © 2024 by ScareStreet.com

This is a work of fiction. Any resemblance to actual persons, living or dead, or actual events is purely coincidental.

Enter the Realm of Terror...

We'd like to take a moment to thank you for your support and invite you to join our VIP newsletter.

Dive deeper into the darkness with exclusive offers, early access to new releases, and bone-chilling deals when you sign up at www.ScareStreet.com.

Let the nightmares begin...

See you in the shadows,
Scare Street

PROLOGUE

The wind blowing in from their left was cold. Donnie acted like it wasn't uncomfortable, not for his sake but for Zack's. He didn't want to look weak in front of his friend, especially after he'd somehow gotten them lost.

He guessed it was after midnight, but there was no way to tell. His phone was as dead as the car they had left behind them. Even his watch didn't work. It didn't make sense, but Zack figured it had to be an electronic disturbance or maybe even something to do with the Proving Grounds they'd passed.

Donnie didn't buy that at all, of course. They were miles and miles from where the nuclear tests had been done, and those also happened at least seventy years earlier. No way that would affect electronics. The whole of Las Vegas would be shut down if that's how it worked. It had to be something else, something smaller and more local. At the end of the day, it didn't matter. They were stuck in the desert, and nothing worked.

If they had stayed on the highway, they would at least be close to traffic. A steady flow came in and out of Vegas, and someone could have found them and helped. Of course, if they'd stayed on the highway, the car probably wouldn't have died in the first place.

Zack suggested going back the way they came, but before everything died, they were much closer to their destination than they would have been if they'd stayed on the main road. Plus, they could see the lights ahead beyond the canyons they were walking toward. The glow had to be Las Vegas. They'd be there soon enough, get a tow truck, and figure out what happened to the car later.

If someone had asked Donnie the day before whether there was a snowball's chance in hell he would abandon the car and walk through the desert at night, he would have said no. But their destination looked so near that he figured it made more sense to keep on than to double back and take the highway.

He had heard that the desert got cold at night. The temperature during the day was close to one hundred degrees. It must have dropped at least forty degrees since sundown, though.

There wasn't a cloud in the sky above them. The stars were like he had never seen them. It was like the sky was somehow closer here than back home. Everything was brighter and clearer; it was amazing. For all the inconvenience of the car dying, it was a hell of a view, and it would make for a great story when they got home. He only wished his phone still worked so he could take a picture.

"At least this was a shortcut," Zack said.

Donnie chuckled and nodded. It had been his idea to follow the road he had found on his GPS, which looked like it would get them to Las Vegas nearly an hour sooner than taking the highway in.

The road they were on now was barely a road at all, just a patch in the desert that someone had driven down before. He figured as long as the GPS was working, it would take them to where they wanted to go. He would have never imagined that the power would go out on everything, and they would have no idea where they were or how much farther they had to go.

"I feel like an idiot, man. I'm sorry," Donnie said.

"It's fine," Zack said.

They'd already had it out in the car, such as it was. They'd been best friends for nearly fifteen years; a wrong turn wasn't going to make them rage at one another or anything. Donnie still felt bad.

If nothing else, getting lost was keeping in the theme of their friendship. They did stupid things together all the time; they had since school. No dare was too dumb for either of them.

For three years now, they had taken a yearly trip to Vegas to party, lose money, and have a good time that neither of them remembered well after it was over. They loved it. This year was already off to an epic start.

"McMasters is going to be pissed," Donnie said.

Their friend, Doug McMasters, was flying in from Michigan. They'd not seen him since the summer after high school, and it was set to be a bit of a reunion weekend. McMasters had meticulously planned everything for months.

"He'll be fine. We'll get him drunk at the Bellagio, and he'll loosen up," Zack said.

"Here's hoping," Donnie replied.

They walked onward, the sand crunching underfoot as they passed craggy rocks and stumpy cacti. Every so often, some movement would catch Donnie's attention, maybe a lizard or some kind of desert mouse, he thought. They never sat still long enough for him to focus on, but it was always low to the ground, in the shadows at their sides.

"What do you think the tow is going to cost?" Donnie asked.

"I don't know. Maybe fifty or so," Zack guessed.

The wind was blowing in harder now, and Donnie suppressed a shiver. It was getting a lot colder than he thought the desert could get. He wished he'd put on his hoodie before they left the car.

The lights of Vegas beckoned them forward, and they began to ascend a hill that led up to a short, gravelly rock face. The chill deepened, and Donnie bore down, forcing up the hill as sand slid underfoot and threatened to cause him to lose his footing.

He was first up the rise, with Zack right behind him, and he stopped once he was upright. He scanned the horizon and opened his mouth to say something, but no words came out. Zack was at his side a moment later, and neither of them moved.

"What the hell?" Zack said.

There were no lights. There was no bustling city. There was no Las

Vegas. Ahead of them, beyond the ridge that they had just climbed, was nothing but rocks, sand, and endless desert.

Donnie was certain that they had both seen the lights. It wasn't a single light in the night. It wasn't headlights from passing cars, or the setting of the sun. It was the extreme, unmistakable bright lights of Vegas. The city was lit up like no place else they had ever been. The lights they were heading toward couldn't have been anything else. But now, there was nothing.

Donnie turned and looked back the way they had come. He could see no sign of the car behind them. Nor could he even see their footprints, as the wind had swept the sand aside and smoothed the desert out.

He remembered that they had angled slightly west while they walked, to head toward the lights they'd seen. But then they had turned again, hadn't they? He tried to remember where they might have started, where the car should have been, or even the road where they broke down. The way back looked the same as the way ahead: just sand. Sand and darkness.

"Where's the car?" he asked.

Zack turned and looked back.

"I can't even see our tracks," he pointed out.

It wasn't just the trail across the desert that was missing, it was everything. There was not a single print to look back on, even their last ones up the hill. Everything was gone.

"You've got to be kidding me," Zack continued. "We're not just a little lost now, we're completely lost. Do you even know what direction we were walking?"

Donnie did not. His phone and watch were dead. Everything was dead. He had no idea how to navigate by the stars. For all he knew, they could have been anywhere now.

"I mean, we have to be close, right? How far was it to Vegas according to the last sign we passed?"

"I don't know," Zack replied. "You were the one driving, man. You're supposed to be watching road signs."

"I don't remember!" he shot back, then tried to stay calm. "I think it was fifty miles? Or twenty, maybe?"

"Fifty or twenty is a big difference," Zack retorted. "That's like a seven-hour walk versus an entire goddamn day."

"I don't remember!" Donnie said again.

"Unbelievable." Zack turned his back on his friend and ran a hand down his face. "We could be losing a whole day, man. That's if we can even find our way back to the road."

"We should keep going. Those lights had to come from somewhere," Donnie suggested.

"What lights? There's nothing there," Zack yelled, pointing into the dark.

"They came from somewhere," Donnie said, getting angry.

"Dude, where? Did Vegas go to bed? It was an illusion or some kind of reflection we can't see at this angle. There's nothing out there to go to."

He didn't wait for a response. Instead, Zack made his way back down the hill, heading back in the general direction they had come.

"You're going back? Really? We don't even know which way we came from. It's pitch black."

"It's better than continuing that way," Zack said.

"It's not! The city is this way. We both saw it!"

"I've followed you enough for one night, Donnie." He continued into the desert.

Donnie said nothing in response.

Zack had spent most of his friendship with Donnie letting things slide and making himself chill when he needed to chill. Donnie was a bit of a perennial idiot, but that was part of his charm. If something could be screwed up, Donnie would screw it up in the most spectacular way possible. He was funny as hell, and Zack loved him to death, but he got on his nerves sometimes. When his screwups affected everyone else, sometimes Zack just needed space. And now that his screwup was putting their lives in danger, Zack had had enough.

He had no idea which way it was to the car, but the highway had to be straight on. It slashed clean across the desert so if he kept walking, he'd find it soon enough.

At the bottom of the hill, a sound like a chicken bone popping out of a joint caused him to flinch. He looked back, expecting to see Donnie stumbling down the hill after him. Instead, he saw nothing at all. Donnie was gone.

"Donnie?"

There was no reply from his friend. Zack stayed still, waiting for Donnie to reappear, but he did not.

"Seriously?" he said softly.

He figured Donnie would relent and join him, not wander off by himself toward the lights that no longer existed.

"Donnie!"

Still no reply. Zack swore and stormed back up the hill.

"You can't just wander into the desert like an idiot. You're going to die out here."

He reached the top of the rise and nearly fell into a hole, catching himself at the last moment and stumbling back a step. The light from the clear sky was barely there, but there was enough of it to make out his surroundings. There was enough light for him to see that the hole at his feet wasn't empty.

Nothing had been there when he was at the top of the hill with Donnie only a few minutes earlier. No hole, and certainly not one with a dark, rumpled shape within.

Zack crouched to get a closer look.

"Donnie?" he said softly.

His friend was on his stomach but not face-down. His head was twisted backward, and a single hole in the center of his forehead leaked a bead of what looked like black fluid in the darkness. But Zack knew it was red. A trail of blood trickled into the sand next to his friend's head.

"Jesus, Donnie!"

He jumped into the hole. He didn't know why; he could see Donnie was dead. But the reality of it was just... not real. It made no sense. How could he have died? How could a hole appear from nowhere in seconds? It was impossible.

Zack crouched next to Donnie's body and touched his friend's neck for a pulse. He could feel the distended flesh, twisted around the wrong way, and wasn't even sure where he would find the artery now that his friend's neck was so badly broken.

The hole in Donnie's head bled slowly, barely a trickle. His eyes were open and unfixed, looking up at nothing. His skin was still warm.

Panic built in Zack's guts as he tried to reconcile what he was seeing with the lack of time, or a cause, for it to have happened. The longer he stayed in the hole looking down at his friend, the more he began to realize that whatever had killed Donnie had to be close by.

The hole was shallow, not a grave so much as a ditch that had been hastily dug. Even crouched down, Zack was not hidden. He could still see the desert all around him. There was nothing but small rocks and random scrub brush. No one was there, not even a coyote.

"Oh my God," he muttered, shaking his head. "Oh, Jesus."

He looked left and right, backward and forward. It was so dark that it was hard to focus on anything, but he saw no movement. He needed to get help. He needed to find another road, or a house, or any place he could call the police.

The wind kicked sand into the hole, creating a faint sprinkling sound as the grains speckled his and Donnie's body. With it came another sound, barely audible, but there. Laughter. Not a raucous, boisterous laughter. Something softer. A gentle chuckling.

Zack's eyes settled on a cluster of rocks not far away. That was where the laughter originated. Even as he watched and saw nothing that could even be mistaken for a person, he heard it again. Low and rough like a man who smoked too much.

The sand crunched and skidded under his feet as Zack ran. He nearly fell down the hill but kept his footing and ran as fast as he could. The faint laughter faded into the night, lost behind him with the body of his friend.

He ran straight from the ridge, making a beeline for what looked like a distant rock formation, barely visible against the backdrop of the black sky. The desert made running hard, and he found himself getting tired while making little progress at low speed, but he didn't stop.

Despite the coolness of the night, sweat ran down his back, and he felt drops beading in his eyebrows and slipping down the sides of his face. He pressed on until exhaustion demanded he slow down. His legs burned and his breath came in painful gasps as he finally slowed to a stop.

The featureless desert had changed little. Sand and rocks and dry, scraggly plants were all he could see.

The faint, raspy laughter started again close by. Zack's breath caught, and he scanned the night, his eyes fixing on a source. Rocks, just a few yards away. Familiar rocks.

He retreated a step and fell backward into the hole, landing atop Donnie's body.

Zack screamed, struggling awkwardly to extricate himself and get off his friend's body. It was impossible. He had run in a straight line. He hadn't even gone up a hill. It was absolutely impossible.

A shadow from the rocks stretched toward him, moving like a slithering snake and growing long though there was nothing to cast it.

Zack turned to run but fell again, this time into a new hole, a deeper hole. It was empty but roughly the same size as the one that held Donnie.

Flattening himself out in the hole, Zack waited. He could not see over the edge, and he held as still and silent as he could. His breaths were still deep and ragged, and he cursed himself. He couldn't help it; he needed to breathe no matter how loud it sounded.

The shadow he had seen did not appear at the lip of the hole. Nothing loomed above him, threatening to do him harm. Slowly, almost painfully, his breathing evened out and grew quiet.

Zack braced himself, his muscles tense as he prepared to sit up and look out. Before he could even lift his head, he heard that sound again. A pop, the sound of a bone snapping. It was not from the night outside, from an unseen place beyond the hole. It came from within the hole, just behind him. And then the soft, dry laughter came again.

The air grew cold, freezing like ice, and Zack screamed.

Somewhere, far away, a coyote answered.

But Zack's cries ended long before the coyote's.

CHAPTER 1
DEAD MEN TELL NO TALES

The preliminary cause of death for both victims had been listed as a gunshot wound to the head. Agent Xander Ventura stood in a charcoal suit under the heat of the Nevada sun, sweat stinging his eyes, and stared down at the first of the two bodies.

"Who said this was a gunshot?" he asked.

It was clearly not a bullet that had hit the man's head. There was no exit wound, though that didn't necessarily preclude a bullet, but that was the least of the issues. There was no swelling at the wound site, puckering of flesh or even tearing at the edges. It was the smoothest wound entry Ventura had ever seen.

The size of the wound was also too large. It was also irregularly shaped, not a perfect circle.

Most notable was the tissue damage around the edges of the entry wound. The flesh was darkened, but not by a burn or a chemical, and it was also very dry. Ventura had no doubt that it was frostbite. Something freezing cold had been shoved into the victim's head, not a bullet.

"Jed. He's on his way. But we Facetimed and he was shown the bodies," came the answer from one of the officers, a younger man named Malcolm. He wore big, mirrored sunglasses that made him look like a highway patrol officer from a movie.

"Facetimed…?" Ventura shook his head. "And who is Jed?"

"Coroner," Malcolm said.

"And he's on his way. Why hasn't he arrived yet? Shouldn't the coroner be one of the first to arrive on a murder scene?"

Malcolm shrugged. "You were coming, we all thought you might want to see them before they were moved."

"How long's he been coroner?" Ventura asked.

He used the end of a pen to pull down the collar of the dead man's shirt. There were handprints on the twisted neck. Frozen ones.

"No idea. Been elected a dozen times over, I think," Malcolm replied.

"Elected," Ventura said to himself. "Is Jed a doctor, Officer Malcolm?"

"What?" Malcolm asked.

Ventura took a photo of the handprints on the victim's neck. Dry ice could cause the damage he saw, but the handprints were not dry ice. Someone with hands at around negative one hundred and ten degrees had twisted the dead man's head backward.

"Does he have a medical license? Did he go to med school?"

"Oh." Malcolm looked for one of the other officers, but no one was nearby. "I mean, he has to, doesn't he? He's a coroner."

"He does not." Ventura got to his feet. "A medical examiner must have medical training. A coroner should but doesn't have to. Why didn't the Las Vegas medical examiner respond to this?"

"Wrong county," Malcolm said. "If they died about four hundred yards east, maybe. But not here."

Ventura said nothing. The two men, Donnie Kent and Zachary Pruitt, were the sixth and seventh bodies to have been found in the desert in the same relatively small area. There were also three missing people whose vehicle was found nearby.

"We figured it was someone being ironic. Or nostalgic? Not sure what word is right to use here," Malcolm said.

"What does that mean?"

"You know. Gunshot to the head, shallow grave in the desert. Like the mob used to do back when they ran Vegas."

He chuckled, and Ventura looked at the body again. An ironic murderer. That was something, maybe.

No one had publicly said the words "serial killer", but it was only a matter of time. The deaths were so far from any population that they had not garnered a lot of attention. The first were thought to have been accidents, hikers who got lost. These two would easily put an end to that belief. No one accidentally twisted their head backward in a makeshift grave after poking a hole in their skull.

Ventura had taken an interest when he had read some of the details of the case. The earlier victims had the same signs of extreme cold on their bodies. Not enough that anyone seemed to care, and now that he knew the coroner was an elected official who was likely not schooled in forensic pathology, it made more sense.

There was not a lot to go on beyond Ventura's initial inspection of the two most recent bodies, and looking at previous crime scene photos, but he had an idea about what happened. He was fairly certain he was looking at the victims of a ghost.

The first victims had only been a month and a half earlier. All so far had been found in the deep desert, miles from Las Vegas. A few ranches and homesteads were nearby, but so far, no suspects had been identified by local police, and no evidence pointed to who it might have been.

It was unlikely anyone would have even discovered the two new bodies if not for a photographer and a model heading down a dusty road to do a photo shoot who'd found the abandoned vehicle, as well as a suspicious flock of vultures.

The latest victims' vehicle was a head-scratcher. The police could not explain it, and Ventura was not sure what might have gone wrong, either. They still had half a tank of gas, the engine was fine, and the battery was fine, so there was no reason to abandon it. Nevertheless, it appeared as though the men had driven out into the desert, stopped the car in the middle of nowhere, got out, and then walked another several hundred yards before they were killed.

The wind had ensured there were no footprints to determine if a third person was with them, but there were no signs of struggle on the victims. The mysterious head wounds had barely bled, another side effect of the extreme cold.

"How far from here was the first crime scene?" Ventura asked.

"Can't be more than five or six hundred yards over that ridge." Malcolm pointed to some rocks.

"What did the nearest resident say when you interviewed him?"

"Who?" Malcolm asked.

Ventura sighed loudly.

"Who lives closest to the spot where we're standing?"

"Oh. The Ross Ranch is over there a ways. I mean, it's still a good clip from here. He never heard anything."

"Is this Ross a suspect?"

"Ross? Nah. My old man and Ross used to play poker. He's a bit of a blowhard, but he's not shooting people in the head in the desert."

Ventura nodded. Sometimes, he forgot that police work in certain parts of the country was a little more rustic than where he was from. There were parts of the world where a person being your dad's poker buddy precluded them from being a murderer. Places where a hole in the head had to be caused by a bullet, because what else would put a hole in somebody's head?

"Do we have a working theory?"

"These two were booked at Caesars, so they were going to Las Vegas, coming in from San Diego. They had another guy booked with them, but we checked, and he's flying in from Michigan, supposed to be touching down any time now. Looks like they left the main road around eleven-thirty, based on credit card receipts from their last gas purchase and distance traveled. We think they drove up that dirt road, left the vehicle, and were murdered up here in the graves where the bodies were found."

Ventura stared at the other man and waited for more. His mirror image stared back at him in Malcolm's glasses, but the younger officer had nothing to add.

"No theory about why they left the road? Why they left the car? Why they came up here? Who killed them?"

"No, sir," Malcolm replied. "It's like one of the previous crime scenes, as you saw in the file. We think it's the same suspect."

"Yes, we think that," Ventura said to himself.

He was hoping for a little more information to go on before he began his investigation. The local cops would not be looking for a ghost, but if they had discovered anything, it could have pointed him in the right direction. If not a motive, then maybe a witness, or something more to the M.O. other than leaving a dead body in the desert. It looked like none of that was in the cards.

With seven bodies already and potentially three more somewhere in the sand, the killer was swiftly racking up a body count. Area police were in no position to solve the crime, or even help anyone else survive.

"What about the first few deaths?" Ventura asked.

"Coyotes," Malcolm said. "Couple of hikers killed by coyotes is what Jed figured."

"He hasn't revised that opinion in light of these recent murders?"

"Well, they were being eaten by coyotes when they were found," Malcolm pointed out as though Ventura were stupid for not acknowledging that.

The agent pulled out his phone and scrolled through his apps.

"Victim one, Jamie Huxley, aged twenty-eight. Six-foot-two, one hundred eighty pounds, construction worker. Victim two, Mark Emmett, aged twenty-seven. Six-foot even, one hundred sixty-seven pounds, worked in construction with Huxley. You're telling me Jed thinks two large, healthy young men wandered into the desert and were both killed by coyotes?"

"You can look at the photos," Malcolm said.

"Malcolm, do you know how many people coyotes have killed in North America?" Ventura asked.

Prior to traveling to the crime scene, Xander Ventura had no idea how many people were killed every year by coyotes, so he had looked up the statistics.

"Agent Ventura—" Malcolm began exasperatedly.

"Ballpark number," Ventura said, cutting him off.

"I don't know. A hundred?" the officer replied.

"No. None. Coyotes have only killed two people in North America since anyone started keeping track. One was a three-year-old back in the eighties. They don't kill full-grown construction workers. It doesn't happen."

"I saw the bodies, agent. I don't know what to tell you."

Ventura sighed. The sun was hot, and he could feel the sweat soaking into his shirt. He wanted to get back to town. He wanted to talk to Jed.

"You like steak, Officer?" he asked.

"Yeah," Malcolm replied.

"You kill the cows yourself?"

"What?"

"Just because you eat food doesn't mean you killed the animal it came from. Where can I find your friend Jed?"

Malcolm gave him the address of the coroner's office, and Ventura wished him a good day. When he got back to his car, he put the air conditioning on full blast and sat there for a moment, waiting for the car to cool down.

He hoped that Officer Malcolm was not an example of the level of law enforcement in the area. Maybe someone had sent him to babysit Ventura as a joke. It wouldn't be the first time that jurisdictional issues had caused him to butt heads with local police. He feared that might not be the case though, and that the investigation was already being mishandled.

Ghosts or not, everyone should have nailed down some basic details by now. Blaming two deaths on coyotes was borderline negligence, incompetence at the very least.

Ventura stared at the map app on his phone that showed him the quickest route to the coroner's office. It was miles from where he was, back down the road he had already traveled, and away from Las Vegas.

He could go there and track down Jed the coroner. He could try to get the man to account for his questionable findings, but it would prove nothing in the end. He would be no closer to finding out why the victims were dead or who had done it.

What little evidence he'd seen had convinced Ventura that the murderer was a ghost. The local cops might run interference or do background checks for him, but they would be of no help to the investigation he needed to conduct. In fact, they would only get in the way. They didn't have any value to add to what he was doing.

With three people still missing, time was not on Ventura's side. Even if they were dead, the ghost was killing at a rapid pace. There would be more victims, and with little to go on, Ventura did not think he could prevent the next murder. He needed someone who could help, someone who knew what they were doing.

Ventura closed the map app and switched over to his contacts before pressing the button to dial the phone.

CHAPTER 2

GO WEST

"Your phone is ringing."

Shane Ryan opened his eyes and stared up at the ceiling of his room.

"The phone."

He blinked but did not roll over or look toward the phone, which he could also hear ringing on the nightstand beside the bed.

"Shane Ryan, your phone is ringing."

He could not see Eloise, but she was standing very close. She must have been having one of her bored days if she was willing to pester him awake.

It was the middle of the afternoon and, to be fair, there was no good reason for him to be sleeping. On the other hand, he had recently been through the wringer and was still recovering. Without any other responsibilities waiting on him, he thought taking a nap in the middle of the day wouldn't have been such a controversial decision. Eloise, it seemed, thought otherwise.

Shane rolled over and reached for the phone. Eloise stood next to the nightstand, her pale flesh looking a little more dead than usual in the dim light of the room.

"It's Agent Xander Ventura," she said.

Shane looked at the phone. Ventura's name and number were displayed on the screen.

"So it is," he agreed.

"Do you think he wants to come for a visit? Herbert seems to like him. You could use more friends."

Shane ignored the ghost and pressed the green button on his phone. "Ventura," he said.

"Ryan, hey. Were you sleeping?"

"No. What's up?"

"I'm in Nevada, and I ran across something the state cops are not equipped to handle. Seven bodies left far out in the desert. Last ones have holes in their heads that are ringed with frostbite. One guy's head was twisted a full one-eighty, and I've got frostbit handprints on the neck."

"So it's a ghost," Shane said. "You cracked the case. Good job."

"I thought so, too. But there are no witnesses, no anything. This is the middle of the desert. Seven victims in a month and a half, plus three missing people. Whoever it is, they're working fast."

"How's a ghost finding victims in the middle of the desert?" Shane asked.

He sat up in bed, rolling his shoulders while Eloise made no attempt to hide her eavesdropping.

"Last guys drove way off the highway and left a perfectly functional car to go for a walk before they were killed. No idea why."

"Who were they?"

"Two friends heading to Vegas. Meeting up with an old high school buddy. First two victims were guys just going for a weekend trip, too. Then three who lived in town coming back from visiting relatives in L.A."

"So, no one who had any reason to wander the desert," Shane said.

"No," Ventura agreed. "No connection or pattern that I can see based on the case reports I've read. All random."

"They weren't all killed the same way?" Shane asked.

"Coyotes got to some of the victims, and the coroner out here seems a little suspect. No one else had holes in their heads, though."

Shane grunted as he planted his feet on the cold floor and yawned. Eloise had not moved and seemed intent on listening to the whole conversation.

"So, you're expecting more victims," he said.

"Seems like nothing's stopping this spirit so far. Not sure what got it started, but it's going full tilt."

"Right," Shane said.

He stood up and stretched his back. His body was riddled with partially healed bruises from a half-dozen fights over the previous several months. He needed to slow down, but that was out of his hands. No one else was slowing down.

"I'm thinking I could use a hand out here," Ventura said finally.

Shane knew the man was calling for help, but it amused him to have the FBI asking him for assistance.

"Sounds like," he replied but said nothing more.

Ventura waited a moment in silence and then scoffed on the other end of the phone.

"Can you help me?" he asked. "This one is beyond my skill set."

Shane chuckled and made his way to the bathroom.

"Text me where you need me to go. I'll let you know when I'm close." He hung up and tossed his phone back on the bed.

"You're going to Las Vegas?" Eloise asked as he left the room. She was kind enough to not follow him into the bathroom.

"Looks like." He closed the door behind him. He took a long shower, letting the hot water loosen up some of the muscles that bound up tight during his sleep, and then tossed some clothes in a duffel bag when he was done.

Downstairs, Eloise had shared his plans with the rest of the household. Carl, the Davis sisters, and Herbert were waiting in the kitchen as he entered. Someone had put water on for coffee. Probably the big ghost.

"Eloise tells us you are heading to Las Vegas," Carl said. "I hear it's a very exciting city."

"You heard that?" Shane poured some coffee into a mug.

"I have. In passing. I do go out sometimes, you know."

"I know." Shane took a sip and looked around the room.

"I've been to Las Vegas a few times. It's an incredible place. I once got paid five thousand dollars just to show up at a man's birthday party," Herbert said.

"Five thousand? Really? That's remarkable," Carl said.

"Yeah, and this was in the seventies, mind you! He was from Texas. Some sort of oil man, and—"

"You guys can go over the finer details of Las Vegas theme parties when I'm gone." Shane cut the ghosts off. "Keep an eye on things. Don't lose your heads."

He finished his coffee, rinsed his cup, and made his way to the front foyer. The dead followed him, offering travel tips as he went.

"You should go first class," Daisy suggested. "I heard it's very elegant."

"It's pricey," Dora added.

"Plus, you're first to die if the plane crashes," Daphne said.

"I'm not flying," Shane said. "Waste of money."

"It's got to be a forty-hour drive," Herbert pointed out. "Won't you get bored?"

Shane guessed the ghost was angling for an invite. This wasn't a road-trip-with-friends kind of journey, though. Besides, the house was safer and more secure with everyone home.

It wasn't that Shane doubted the security of the house, but ever since Thomas Coulson had made off with Carl's remains once, Shane had it in the back of his head that something could still surprise him. Coulson had been impossible to predict. Who knew what else might have been out there?

"I'll be fine. Keep an eye on things while I'm gone," Shane said to no one in particular.

He left the ghosts behind and made his way to the car, tossing his duffel bag in the trunk. It had been years since Shane had been to Las Vegas, and he wasn't enthused about going back. He understood the city's appeal to others, but it was not his cup of tea. Too bright, too loud, and too crowded with people who thought the city gave them a license to be idiots. A ghost that murdered random targets was not a good addition.

By the time Shane was on I-90 West, he had gotten a series of texts from Ventura giving him locations of the bodies, details of their deaths, and the hotel where the agent was staying.

The idea of booking a hotel room occurred to him only then, but he shrugged it off. There was nothing if not an abundance of hotel rooms in the city, and he didn't want to stay at the kind of place that wanted people to book their rooms in advance on the internet. He wanted somewhere under the radar and away from the Strip. Quiet and unassuming was his preference.

Past Indiana, the scenery started blurring together. Shane reached Omaha and realized he had been on the road for close to thirty hours straight. The urge to find a room for a night was there, but he felt like he was already so close to where he was going that there was no point stopping now. He could force himself to do another ten hours. What was the worst that could happen?

He shaved a few hours off his trip by ignoring the odd speed limit. It was the middle of the night when he crossed the border into Nevada, and around 3 AM when the lights of Las Vegas pushing back against the night sky finally came into view.

Las Vegas was never off, one of the things Shane didn't like about it. It never knew how to shift down a gear and catch its breath. Everything had to be more. Louder, brighter, bigger, ghastlier. There was too much of everything. It seemed as though the ghost in the desert had taken that to heart. More, more, and more.

Shane avoided the Strip and drove several blocks away from anything that blinked, strobed, or flashed. He passed a half-dozen hotels before settling on an off-white motel with a vintage sign out front that read Golden Gate Towers. There were six floors in each of the would-be towers, and it looked like no one had bothered to paint the exterior since Elvis had a residency.

There were two cars in the parking lot and a dumpster that looked like it hadn't been emptied in well over a month, with trash piling out into the parking lot. A trio of ghosts huddled together under the lot's lone working light, crouched low to the ground and playing cards.

Shane pulled in next to the spirits, none of whom raised their heads at his presence, and rolled down the window. He had never seen a spirit deck of cards, but they had one and were in the middle of a game of poker.

"This place worth staying at?" he asked.

The ghost dealing the cards peered up at him. He looked positively ancient like he had died in his late nineties, with a scraggly beard and mustache stained yellow around his mouth with tobacco. Blood flowed from his ears and the corners of his eyes.

"Who the hell are you?" the spirit asked.

"Deal the cards," one of the others said.

"Just passing through, looking for a quiet place to stay," Shane said.

The impatient gambler looked over his shoulder. He was younger than the dealer by a few decades and would have outweighed him by at least two hundred pounds.

"You one of them ghost guys?" he asked.

The third ghost, a woman with messy hair and broken teeth, finally looked at him as well.

"Doesn't look like one," she said.

"I don't know what that is," Shane replied. "Just need a place where I can trust no one's breaking into my room to steal my things."

"You mind, buddy? We're in the middle of something," the younger male ghost said.

All three returned to their game, and Shane decided it'd be worth his time to stay there. The ghosts could be helpful if he needed them. But, more importantly, if they were permanent fixtures, then the hotel probably didn't have cockroaches or bed bugs.

Shane parked away from the dumpster and headed into the office to check in. He asked for something on the first floor, but the clerk at the counter told him the only rooms left were on the sixth floor. Shane didn't argue, even though there were only two other cars in the parking lot. He took his room at the top of the western tower and headed upstairs.

The room smelled musty, and the air conditioning blew air that was inexplicably warmer than what was already in the room, but he didn't care that much. There were no signs of bed bugs or roaches, and that was all that mattered. He'd call Ventura when he woke up.

CHAPTER 3

THE WHISPERING SANDS

"Did you pay sixty dollars for this?"

Shane stared across the table at Ventura. They were at the Wynn Casino, and the agent had loaded a plate with scrambled eggs, breakfast sausage, and bacon, along with a pile of fresh fruits.

"Each." Ventura nodded.

Shane had a coffee and indulged the other man by taking some crispy bacon and sourdough toast. He was not going to eat sixty dollars' worth of breakfast at a casino buffet.

"You eat like this all the time?" Shane asked.

Ventura shrugged, chewing on a sausage.

"Fast metabolism. Plus, I work out a lot. You can use the gym here if you want. As my guest."

"I don't go to the gym." Shane wrinkled his nose.

Ventura stopped eating and looked at him suspiciously.

"Ever?"

"I have basic equipment at home, that's it."

Ventura nodded and had another bite of the sausage.

Shane had called Ventura just after sunrise, and the two had met at the casino at eight. The agent had reserved them a table and brought some files and crime scene photos with him.

"You learn anything since we last spoke?" Shane asked.

Ventura grunted, nodding as he leafed through some files.

"Missing family did the same thing as our latest victims. Car left the road for some reason, and it looks like they abandoned it in the desert even though it had a quarter tank of gas. Battery was fine. No pings on their phones since they vanished."

"Still no witnesses?"

"It's dead out there. Closest I have is a rancher who the cops assure me is a great guy."

"And we're buying that?" Shane asked.

"No, but I haven't had a chance to question him yet. No history of anything in the area unless you go back about sixty years, and then it's *maybe* mob hits in the desert, but nothing confirmed. No bodies have ever been pulled up there, but it's on a map that covers about a hundred square miles of where mob hits might have taken place."

"That's a bit of a range," Shane said.

"Yeah. Locals are not moving on this like it's anything important. You'd think they dig up corpses all the time the way they're disinterested. Chalked up the first two to coyote attacks. I'm waiting on a coroner's report on the latest two, and I've asked the Las Vegas ME to look into them as a favor, but I doubt forensics is going to steer us anywhere we need to go."

"It won't," Shane agreed. "Not a lot of ghosts out there leaving DNA or fingerprints."

"But." Ventura shoveled a large amount of eggs into his mouth, which caused him to take a preposterously long pause before speaking again. "I found something weird."

"Which was?"

"The car driven by our latest victims. I checked it out two days ago. Locals had impounded it, so I gave it a once-over. Engine starts like a charm, more than half a tank of gas. Nothing weird or out of place inside. Guys left their luggage in the back, and some food, one of them even left their phone. How many people you know leave their phone behind, especially in an emergency, to go for a walk?"

"These days? Not many," Shane said.

"Locals didn't report anything weird, but I checked the radio when the car came on. I figure two guys on the road have to be listening to something. Nothing preset. No favorite channels. Full, basic, factory radio. But the victim had owned the car for four years."

He stared at Shane with a strangely excited expression. It was the most animated Shane had seen Ventura since they met. The other times they had worked together, Ventura was behind the eightball and reacting to things he had never planned or experienced. Now that he was running the show, he was getting into it. And he was clever.

"The battery died, and the electronics were reset to factory settings," Shane said.

"Right. But the battery wasn't dead when I got to it."

"Ghost killed the power."

Shane had experienced ghosts interfering with electronics. Sometimes, it was just enough to kill the lights in a room. But killing a whole car and wiping the preset functions wasn't too much of a stretch.

"They were lured off the road somehow. I don't know. Hell, maybe the driver thought it was a shortcut. But the ghost catches sight and drains the car. That explains why there hadn't been a call for help, and why one of them left their phone behind. Nothing worked. They either ran for their lives or maybe they saw something and went toward it, hoping to get help. Only things didn't go as planned," Ventura said.

"Plausible," Shane agreed. "Could be how all the victims were lured in. Dead car, dead phone. Might have been an illusion that they were still on the highway."

"Right," Ventura said. "Just... why these people? Why now? This ghost just appeared a few weeks ago, and there was never anything like this anywhere before now that I can find."

"When you're done with your sixty-dollar eggs, let's go for a drive, see what we can find," Shane suggested.

"You're seriously just eating toast?" Ventura asked.

"And bacon." Shane held up an overcooked piece.

He took a bite while Ventura finished his meal, and then they headed out, taking Ventura's car.

They drove to the latest crime scene first, with Ventura following directions on his phone to a pin he'd dropped on a map. Shane didn't point out the irony of relying on a virtual map after having established that a ghost had killed the victims' electronics.

The drive took longer than Shane expected. He was under the impression it was very close to the city, but it turned out to be miles beyond the city limits and out in the open country. The land was desolate and mostly empty, and the few homes he saw were lonely and forgotten in the middle of nowhere.

The landscape was dotted with mountain ranges, rocky outcroppings, scrub, and cactus, but mostly sand. The sky looked so big once they were out on the road that it was stunning to sit back and just look at it all. It was the same sky that you'd find anywhere in the world, but for some reason, over the open desert, it looked like it stretched on forever.

Ventura went over the details of the case as he knew them, along with some of his speculations. Shane listened, watching the desert pass by. There were few ghosts out in the Nevada desert, fewer than he would have guessed given the reputation.

Surely there had been plenty of people who died out in the lonely stretches over the years. Knowing what he knew of ghosts, Shane would have expected most to have congregated near the highways where they could see people. That was not the case. He saw only one spirit after they left Las Vegas, a grizzled-looking man who must have come from the frontier days, walking with his head down.

Ventura took a right turn onto what Shane didn't realize was a dirt road until he focused on it a little more intently and was able to discern the faintest runnels in the dirt representing old tire tracks, barely visible beneath a layer of shifting dust.

"This where they turned?" Shane asked.

"Yeah. Car was parked a few hundred yards up the road here."

"Even if there wasn't a ghost, this was a bad idea."

"Can't argue with that," Ventura said.

He came to a stop at a spot that would have been nondescript if not for some police tape and parking cones that had been set up. Both men got out, and Shane kept his head down, avoiding the blinding sun in the cloudless sky.

It was still early, but the temperature was already flirting with triple digits. At the height of the day, the desert would be unbearable.

"I need to start dealing with ghosts farther North." Shane looked at the area where the car had been. Nothing in the sand was out of the ordinary. There was no way to even tell a car had been parked there.

"The bodies were found up this way. It's a bit of a hike, but I figured you'd want to retrace the whole path," Ventura said.

"Yeah, lead on." Shane thought it would have been a more pleasant trip later in the evening, but he wasn't there to waste time.

They trudged through sand, sometimes loose, and sometimes hard-packed like stone. Ventura checked his phone at regular intervals to make sure they were still on track. The desert offered nothing but stones and dry-looking plants and the occasional lizard.

Shane saw no sign of any spirit as they walked. There was nothing close by, not even movements in the distance or from the corner of his eyes. Whatever was out there, whatever had killed those two men and the others that had gone missing before them, it wasn't in the area. If it was, it could not have cared less about Shane and Ventura being in its territory.

They reached the crime scene, another nondescript spot at the top of a ridge, and Shane crouched next to the marked-off areas where what had once been shallow graves sat empty. With the wind and sand, they had mostly filled in and were a little more than soft indentations in the otherwise flat ground.

"No sign of any tool used to dig these holes. They were deeper before, obviously. Nothing in them besides the bodies. No fabric or anything unrelated to the corpses. Not that I would have expected otherwise. If I had to guess, the ghost dug them by hand and dropped the men inside," Ventura said.

Shane grunted, taking a handful of the hot sand and letting it run through his fingers. Ghosts didn't technically dig holes by hand, but he understood what the other man meant.

He stood and looked around. From the ridge they were on, he could just barely make out cars on the distant highway. Little spots of reflected light moved like ants in the distance. Their car reflected the sunlight back at him as well. In the dark, however, it would have looked like they were in the middle of nowhere.

Shane turned his back on the way they had come and looked out at what might lay ahead. The men were walking toward something. It stood to reason that they had a destination in mind. From where he was standing, however, there was nothing. The path the men had taken, if they'd kept on in a straight line, led toward some very distant mountains and nothing else.

There were a couple of possibilities for what had happened. They could have been running from something and were not concerned with where they were going, just getting away. The other possibility was that they were tricked into thinking they were heading toward something. Each one was reasonable, and neither gave him much more insight into what he was looking for.

"Where were the other bodies found?" Shane asked.

"That way." Ventura pointed into the distance beyond a ridge. "About five hundred yards. Those were the men thought to be eaten by coyotes. And the other three were back that way about the same distance."

He pointed to Shane's left, but Shane could see nothing that looked different from the rest of the desert. It didn't matter. He was certain there would be nothing to see.

"Okay." Shane crouched again. He planted a finger in the sand and made a circle. "This is us and the crime scene here."

"Sure," Ventura said.

"And this is the coyote guys," Shane continued, making another mark a short distance away. "And then your third group of victims here."

He made a third mark and looked at it.

"Close to eight hundred yards between coyotes and the others, give or take," he said.

Ventura nodded.

"I think so."

"So, we've got some range to work with here. This ghost is only wandering a mile or so from home. This covers about half of his territory with just these two kills. Let's say he can reach the road, and that's how he's lured people in, that means his upper range is about here." Shane drew a line at the top of his makeshift map.

"So, he has to be based in here somewhere." Ventura gestured to a swath of sand.

"Somewhere. What's in this area? Any houses? Caves?"

"Ranch." Ventura poked his finger into the sand to indicate its location. "The one I told you about. Plus maybe five trailers and a couple of abandoned houses. As for caves, I have no idea. Got to be some."

"We can look for those after. The ranch has to be our first stop."

CHAPTER 4

HOUSE OF SECRETS

Shane's plan to cross the sand and sneak up behind the ranch did not align with Ventura's, it turned out.

"We have to play this by the book," the agent said. "This is an open murder investigation. We can't be trespassing or breaking and entering."

"We can't?" Shane asked as they made their way back to the car.

"No, we can't," Ventura repeated.

"Let me put the emphasis on that differently. *We* can't?" he said.

Ventura sighed and shook his head.

"You're helping me on this case, remember? I help you, we do things your way. You help me, we obey the law."

"Yeah, but no one has to know I'm with you if I go in."

"Someone's going to know. I'll know," Ventura said. "I'm still an FBI agent. We can do this the right way."

"Do ghosts have rights?" Shane asked. "If you don't Mirandize them, does that matter?"

"Don't make fun of me," Ventura said as he unlocked the car.

Shane chuckled and got in on the passenger side. The inside of the vehicle was stifling, and this stale, hot air took some of the wind out of his sails when it came to giving Ventura a hard time about his approach.

He understood the need to follow rules when it came to a living criminal. If the murderer had been a real man, there would be a reason to follow procedures to make sure everything played out the way it should. But this was a ghost. There wouldn't be a trial, or prison time, or anything like that.

Ventura was more of a big-picture guy when it came to the situation. Shane was worried about the ghost. If someone living was involved like an accomplice or even someone using the ghost as an active weapon, they could be dealt with in the same manner. Ventura didn't see it that way.

In cases where they had worked together in the past, Ventura always had to strike a balance between dealing with the inexplicable and accounting for what he was doing. Shane had not asked for many details, but he understood that Ventura had a way of jumping through hoops and twisting the truth to hide details that the FBI was not ready to handle. It wasn't as though the man could write a report blaming murders on someone who was already dead.

"By the book," Shane agreed. "If we can."

Ventura looked at him suspiciously but didn't say anything about the caveat. Shane was more than willing to follow the law if it didn't interfere with what needed to be done, there were just instances when the law fell short. He wasn't going to respect any rules of trespassing if it would cost him an opportunity to put an end to a ghost that was killing people.

The ranch was not an easy place to find if you didn't know where you were going. To say it was off the beaten path was something of an understatement. They returned to the highway off the dirt road and traveled in a wide arc back to the way they had come. From there, it was down another series of side roads, each one less populated than the one before it, until they reached a dirt driveway that was bordered on either side by gnarled trees. Had they not been there to mark it, there would have been no way to know they were headed in the right direction.

"Looks like someone likes privacy." Ventura slowed to a stop in front of a gate set into a fence that was more for show than security.

Shane got out of the car and approached the waist-high metal gate, undoing a latch and pushing it open. Ventura frowned at him but shrugged.

"It's not breaking and entering; there was no lock. How else do we get in?" he asked.

The agent said nothing, and they continued their drive. In time, the road dipped, and below, in a valley, they found their destination. The ranch was a wide property with a long house surrounded by several outlying buildings that ranged from small sheds to full barns. Another fence enclosed everything, and a line of trees, struggling against the desert and its inhospitable climate, concealed much of the property beyond the buildings.

Shane had spent little time on ranches in his life, but this one lived up to any stereotype he had expected from movies. The main house was spread out such that someone on one side of the house could have screamed at the top of their lungs and a person on the other side would never have heard them.

Each window had quaint shutters, and there was a wooden archway over the road indicating they had just come to the Boulder Creek Ranch. There was even an ancient tractor broken down on the front lawn with a wagon wheel and some other decorative touches around it. Shane wondered if they offered hayrides.

Ventura pulled to a stop in front of the house next to the covered porch held aloft by big, raw timber columns. There were two trucks and a car parked outside on the driveway in front of a garage. Alongside them was a cherry red nineteen fifty-nine Cadillac Eldorado with fins on the back and plates that read "BOSSROSS".

Ventura took a moment to admire the car while Shane paused to listen for any sounds of life. Nothing came from inside the building or anywhere else on the property that he could tell.

Someone had taken the time to landscape the area with shrubs and cacti that would thrive in the climate. They lined the path from the drive to the walkway and accented the porch and the front of the house near the windows. All of it looked a little sickly and anemic, however, like whoever's job it was to maintain the garden had given up some time ago.

Ventura rang the doorbell while Shane hung back a step, looking at the windows and the front of the house for any sign of ghosts.

It took several minutes and another ring of the doorbell before any indication of a response was forthcoming. Shane heard heavy footfalls from within the house coming toward the door. Two locks clicked before the door pulled open.

The man on the other side was older than Shane, probably in his sixties, but built like a linebacker. He had broad shoulders and a square head half-hidden on a wide-brimmed cowboy hat. He wore a plaid shirt, blue jeans, and cowboy boots as though he'd bought a cowboy starter kit at the mall.

"Help you?" The man had an accent that sounded a little more Southern than Nevada.

He stared out at Ventura and then Shane before returning his attention to the agent. The man's face was craggy and weatherbeaten like he'd seen a few too many days under the sun without his hat on, and his eyes were in a permanent squint under thick, smoke-gray brows.

"My name is Agent Xander Ventura. I'm with the FBI."

Ventura held up his badge and ID, and Shane held back a laugh. Ventura was very much like a Hollywood cop when he flipped his credentials open. Shane wondered if he realized it. Or if he'd practiced it.

"We're investigating some murders in the desert nearby, and I wonder if I might ask you some questions, Mr...?"

The man stared and chuckled dryly.

"Nothing to do with me," he answered.

"We're just looking to gather some background, see if maybe you saw or heard anything—"

"Nope." The man cut him off.

"I didn't even tell you when it happened." Ventura's smile was wide and polite.

"And it don't matter none. Never saw nothing, never heard nothing. Close the gate on your way out."

The man moved to close the door, but Ventura laid a hand on it, remaining casual.

"I'm sorry, I never caught your name," he said.

The man smiled, and his teeth were stained from years of too much smoking or coffee, or both.

"I never told you, Mr. Agent Xander Ventura."

"Would you mind telling me your name, sir? For my records?"

The man sighed, and his lip curled. He smirked, and for a moment Shane was certain the man was just going to push Ventura aside and close the door, but instead, he offered a half-hearted shrug and relented.

"Ross. Bennet Ross," the man said. "Have a nice day."

Ventura had not taken his hand off the door yet, so Ross' effort to close it again failed.

"Would you mind if I had a look around your property? We have reason to believe a suspect might have come through this way."

Ross dropped his eyes and looked at Ventura's hands.

"Don't see a warrant there, fella," he replied.

"No, I don't have a warrant, Mr. Ross. Was just asking in the hopes you might want to help."

"Tell you what. Come back with a warrant and some probable cause, and you can search my property all you like."

Instead of closing the door, he pulled it open wider, causing Ventura's hand to slip off it. Without another word, he slammed it shut in the agent's face, and then the two locks clicked inside once more. The sound of heavy boots walking away from the door followed shortly after.

"You're good at this," Shane said.

Ventura frowned, taking a step back out into the sun and looking over the house.

"That was rude, right?" he asked.

"He's not easily charmed by a man with a badge, I guess."

"Most people aren't." Ventura walked the length of the house to the farthest wall. Where the house ended, a privacy fence made of six-foot wooden planks began, each one aligned flush to the next, leaving no gaps for viewing.

"You spend much time on ranches?" the agent asked.

"What do you think?" Shane replied.

Ventura pointed to the fence.

"That's not your typical ranch fence. More of a suburban, 'I hate my neighbors watching me in my pool' sort of fence. Only Ross has no neighbors, so what's he need a privacy fence for?"

"Hates FBI agents watching him in his pool?" Shane stood on his toes to look over the edge.

The side of the house was more scrub and sand, and then a line of Joshua and Mesquite trees dense enough to hide whatever lay beyond. A pair of security cameras were mounted on the edge of the roof above their heads and at the far end of the wall near the trees. Shane smiled at the nearest of them.

"Someone's probably watching." Shane nodded to one.

Ventura looked up and straightened his jacket.

"Well, we're just having a friendly look around."

He headed back to the car with Shane at his side. More cameras dotted the property, most on the house, but a couple mounted on the garage and a shed just beyond it. The barn they had seen from the top of the valley was likely outfitted the same. Mr. Ross liked to know what was happening on his property.

"We leaving to get a warrant?" Shane asked.

"Ross doesn't own the desert around his property," Ventura said. "Figure we could go for another walk."

"That's not bending the rules?" Shane asked.

Ventura laughed.

"I'm not a meter maid, Ryan. You do what you need to do to stop the monsters right up to the line without stepping over. No one gives you hell for putting in effort."

"Good to know," Shane said.

Ventura started the engine and looked at the ranch in the rearview mirror as they pulled away from the property.

"I didn't have this guy high on my list of suspects before, to be honest. But he's pushing himself up now."

"Yeah, he's up to something," Shane agreed. "Just let me know when it's time to step over that line."

CHAPTER 5

BEYOND THE LINE

Once Ross' ranch was out of sight, Ventura turned the car into the desert, sending up a cloud of dust and debris behind them as they drove. Bits of gravel pinged off the car's frame and created a rattling roar under the vehicle that made hearing much else inside the car nearly impossible.

Shane focused on the landscape, scanning from rocks to trees to cacti looking for anything out of the ordinary. There was nothing.

They drove up a ridge to the east of the valley that led down into Ross' property and were soon within sight of a canyon that led into a rocky basin. Ventura drove slowly and then came to a stop in the shade of an oblong boulder, turning off the car and getting out.

"We should be able to get a decent look at things from here, maybe head down that slope over there to get closer if we need to." He pointed to a rocky path that led down toward the ranch.

Shane stood in the full light of the sun, feeling the heat on his skin, and breathing in the dry, hot air. He stood still for barely a heartbeat, and a quick swirl of cool air gusted his way from the shadow of the boulder.

He turned his head to look, but nothing was there. Ventura had not noticed it and was making his way toward the ranch. Shane stayed where he was, looking at the rock with its jagged edges and pockets of darkness that its uneven surface hid. Nothing moved, and nothing looked back at him. The air stayed hot and still, and he eventually turned away.

"You ever come across something like this?" Ventura asked as Shane caught up with him.

They headed down the precarious, stony path toward the valley, and

Ross' ranch came into view. The property was surrounded by a fence but, from their vantage point, much of the rear was now visible, at least on the eastern side. The land Ross owned was expansive, and the fence vanished far to the south while the western side was not visible.

"A ranch in Nevada? No," Shane said.

"No. Someone covering for a ghost. Or using them to do their dirty work," Ventura clarified.

Shane squinted and looked into the valley. Behind the Mesquite and Joshua trees were smaller, fenced-in plots at the rear of the ranch house adjacent to the large barn and some of the other outbuildings. They looked almost like kennels that dog breeders might set up, enclosed by a mesh fence on the sides and the top.

"All the time," Shane said. "Remember, I was nearly killed a few times by mercenaries who used ghosts as weapons? Was tossed into a prize fight in front of a gambling audience against a ghost once. And you were there for the Harvesters."

"That was different," Ventura said. "This guy doesn't seem like a sport hunter."

"No," Shane agreed.

He didn't think Ross was like the Harvesters or the Reapers he'd met overseas. If anything, he seemed like someone who just didn't want to be involved. But he probably knew something. He just had that stink about him.

"He could just be running a meth lab, too," Shane added after a moment. "Doesn't want the FBI around."

"Didn't smell like a meth lab," Ventura said. "No ventilation, either."

He gestured to the rooftops as though that explained everything. Shane shrugged. He was not up to date on the HVAC needs of meth labs, so he took the other man's word for it.

The path toward the ranch dipped into another small canyon from which they would have to follow another ridge up farther to the south.

The sand and gravel lining it showed that, whenever it got rainy in the area, the canyon became a river. The pattern was a dead giveaway of flowing water that headed north to south, though it had been a long time since any water ran in that direction.

They had walked nearly twenty paces through the dry riverbed and followed it around a slight bend in the rock when they were forced to stop. A ghost sat a short distance away, slumped among a scattering of boulders.

Shane glanced up to the top of the ridge above them and could see where the rocks had fallen away in the past. It looked like it had been a minor landslide, with a small portion of the cliff slipping away and piling up in the dry riverbed below.

The ghost was thin and dirty. His clothes were ragged as though they had been discarded and forgotten for years before he put them on. The original color had been replaced by a dull, muddy brown. His hair matched, matted and plastered to his head with caked-on mud and filth.

Although he was not looking up at them, Shane could see the ghost's face was marred by numerous contusions. Cuts, scrapes, bruises, and swollen lumps covered every inch of exposed flesh. He looked as though he had gone down a mountain face-first.

The torn and dirty sleeves on the ghost's jacket hung loose at the wrists. He had no hands, just the raw and ragged stumps of where they used to be. Whatever removed them had not been clean and was likely very painful. They looked to have been sawed off or even chewed, with sharp, splintered bone fragments protruding from the meaty remnants left behind.

Ventura stopped, his body rigid, and his muscles tensing. Shane continued forward, stopping several feet in front of the ghost.

"Hey. You been around here long?" he asked.

The ghost lifted his head. One of his eyes was grossly swollen and blood red; the other had a scratch that sliced through the center and continued down his cheek.

He had no answer for Shane, nor did he even reply. A look of rage spread across the spirit's face almost instantly and he was on his feet, using the stumps on his wrist to push off, propelling him toward the two living men.

The ghost shrieked like an animal and tried to stab Shane in the gut with the spear-like bone in his right arm. Shane sidestepped the attack, easily pushing the ghost aside.

Ventura was on the ghost quickly, producing an iron baton from inside his suit jacket and bringing the metal rod down in a crushing blow atop the ghost's head. Had the man still been alive, his skull would have cracked from the force. Instead, the ghost vanished in a blink, and Ventura stumbled. The momentum of the swing nearly took him off balance when the iron passed unobstructed through its target.

Before either of the men could say anything, the ghost reappeared, scrambling out from behind the boulders he had previously been sitting on. The speed of his return meant that his haunted item was somewhere within the scattered rocks. He had chosen to haunt the area near the item rather than venture farther away, something not uncommon among the dead.

"Might want to fall back for this one," Shane suggested to Ventura.

As fast as Ventura might have been with his iron baton if he was only banishing the ghost to a pile of rocks a few feet away, it wouldn't be that helpful in a fight. Shane put himself between the agent and the ghost and waited for the spirit's attack.

The ghost was slower this time and more cautious, but not by much. Once he saw that Shane was taking point in the fight, the ghost ignored Ventura and came at Shane again.

The ghost wielded the splintered bones of each wrist like short blades. Without hands, however, his reach was severely diminished. When he came in with a second attempt at a gut stab, Shane's fist collided with the spirit's jaw, snapping his head sharply to one side.

The ghost snarled a wet and gurgling sound and dropped low, tackling Shane to the dusty ground. He jabbed a stump into Shane's thigh but couldn't get the leverage to puncture his jeans.

Shane took the ghost's head in his hands and jammed a thumb into the already-ruined eye. The ghost shrieked and shook like a wet dog, inadvertently forcing Shane's thumb deeper until the eyes burst, leaking cold wetness down his wrist.

As the ghost reared back, Shane rolled them over. He pulled his thumb free of the ghost's skull, the fierce cold biting into his flesh, and slammed his elbow hard into the ghost's face, breaking its nose and flattening it to the side of the dead man's cheek.

"Just asking a few questions; you didn't have to be difficult," he explained.

The ghost snarled, and Shane saw the inside of his mouth for the first time. Someone had cut out the ghost's tongue, another rough hack job like the hands. He couldn't have spoken even if he wanted to.

Shane held fast as the ghost writhed and fought against him. There would not be a peace between them. He leaned into it, forcing his weight down as he squeezed the spirit's head.

The ghost bucked and struggled, but Shane had the better position and more leverage. He forced his weight down and brought his hands together, crushing the ghost's skull. It collapsed inward, but only for a moment. As the head gave way, the body exploded outward, and Shane was thrown back a few yards.

"Ryan!"

Ventura's warning cry had not been specific enough to make Shane even lift his head. He remained on his back, staring up at the big Nevada sky and catching his breath when he felt something latch onto his ankle.

"The hell are you doing?" Shane looked up at the FBI agent, who was forcefully dragging him across the dry riverbed.

To Shane's right, one of the boulders had been knocked loose in the rockslide from which the ghost had appeared. Though it was not preposterously large, the rock weighed at least several hundred pounds, and it was rolling quickly toward the spot where Shane had fallen.

Ventura pulled hard and fell backward, yanking Shane with him and out of the path of the rolling rock that would have otherwise crushed him. The agent fell on his backside as Shane sat up, looking over to the rockslide and the shattered remnants of a skeleton clothed in rags.

The ghost's body had been trapped beneath the stone. His spirit had been tied to it, so the destruction of the ghost caused the destruction of the bones, which set the rock free. Had it not been for the missing hands and tongue, Shane would have thought the ghost had died in the rockslide. Someone had made him disappear in the desert and used a forced rockslide to hide the body.

"Thanks." Shane looked at the rock that had narrowly missed him.

"Yeah. No problem." Ventura sat up and dusted off his suit. "That was something."

Shane got up and inspected the newly exposed remains. The tattered clothing matched the spirit he had just dispatched. It must have been out in the desert for years.

"Think that was our guy?" Ventura asked.

"No hands," Shane reminded him. Their victims had frostbitten handprints. This ghost was just a wayward spirit. A victim, perhaps. Someone had had a beef with him to remove his hands and tongue.

"Maybe Ross knows something about it," Ventura guessed, trying in vain to clean the dry sand from the back of his pants.

"Maybe. Hands and tongue missing looks like punishment for something. Stealing. Snitching. Both, I guess," Shane said.

"Weird to have it so close to his house, though," the FBI agent pointed out.

"Unless he just doesn't care. Or doesn't know who is being killed out here," Shane said.

Ventura stood at Shane's side, looking down at the scattered bone fragments and then the iron baton in his hand.

"Is there anything better than this for fighting them? For someone like me?" he asked.

Shane looked at the baton. There were only so many ways the living could interact with the dead. In a fight, the options were limited.

"I haven't seen much that can harm a ghost. Not much you want to try, anyway. Lead and salt hold them well enough. Iron repels. Selenium can trap them, but if you touch possessed selenium, you become possessed. I don't recommend it," Shane told him.

"How do you do it?" Ventura asked.

It was a question everyone asked eventually. Usually ghosts, but sometimes the living if they saw what he could do and understood what it meant.

"Just can. Not sure why. Or how."

"Beatrix could do it too. So it's not just you," Ventura said.

Shane nodded.

"Not many others I've met can. Not sure it's a skill you can learn."

Ventura balled his hand into a fist and looked at it.

"Would be something if I could, though."

"Easy there, Tyson. One fight at a time."

"Yeah," Ventura conceded. "Our killer's still out there."

CHAPTER 6

ROADBLOCKS

Shane picked at the remains of the body in the rocks. The destruction of the spirit had damaged it greatly, but remnants of clothing were left behind, and something more.

"What do you make of this?" He lifted an old, partially unraveled rope stuck to chunks of a thicker fabric.

"Looks like a blanket. Curtains, maybe?" Ventura inspected the fabric. The legs of the skeleton were still bound up in it. The body had been wrapped and then tied with the rope. His death was not a hasty murder in the desert, it was a body dump with the rockslide used to cover it up.

"Decades old." Shane crushed the fabric in his fist and watched it crumble and flake away. "Has to predate Ross, right?"

"Probably," Ventura said. "Not sure what that means, though."

"Maybe nothing," Shane said. "Could just be a coincidence. Could be what you said before. This part of the desert has a reputation. Old mob hits, that sort of thing. Maybe a lot of people disappeared out here and someone's still doing it."

Ventura nodded, turning his back on the scattered and partially destroyed remains and looking up at the ridge on the other side.

"Let's head to Ross' and see what's there. Maybe there's a connection we can make."

He led the way out of the narrow canyon and up a precarious path across jutting rocks and too-small footholds up to the top of the ridge on the far side. From there, it was an easy slope down to the valley and Ross' fence line with whatever secrets it hid.

By the time Shane reached the top of the ridge behind Ventura, it was clear that their plan was going nowhere. Ross was behind the ranch, standing with a pair of other men in cowboy hats and nearly identical outfits.

There was a trio of fenced-in pens behind the ranch house, adjacent to the barn. Each one looked like a set of batting cages at an amusement park, only nothing was inside except for more fencing. They could have held several dozen people each, but all Shane saw was sand and chain link.

Whatever the pens had held, if anything, had been cleared out. The only thing Shane saw clearly in the yard was Bennet Ross, facing the two men on the ridge. He waved at Ventura and Shane, and the two men with him turned to face them as well.

"So much for sneaking around," Ventura said.

"Those are good cameras," Shane said, squinting. He saw small, black blocks reflecting faint glimmers of light on the corners of every outbuilding, fencepost, and the empty cages. Ross had dozens of cameras on his property.

"Probably saw us coming before we went down into the canyon, cleared out whatever was back there. But what the hell is he keeping in cages?"

"You can keep all kinds of things in cages," Shane pointed out.

"Our killer?" Ventura asked.

"Don't need three cages to hold one ghost. Especially if you keep letting it out to kill random people. It's got to be something else."

"Well, unless he's the Tiger King of Nevada, I have no idea. I've never seen a setup like this," the agent said.

"Neither have I. Doesn't make sense as a ghost pen, unless it's a graveyard and the bodies are all buried inside, but that doesn't look like a cemetery to me."

Shane was stumped, but he also realized they were getting ahead of themselves. Ross was a rancher, and he didn't like the FBI, but that didn't necessarily make him a ghost-wielding murderer. He could have been an anti-government type, a drug dealer, or a regular murderer who didn't rely on the supernatural. Hell, he might not have been a criminal at all, not that Shane believed that.

"I feel like an idiot standing here," Ventura said. The three men on the ranch were too far away to see clearly, but they were still watching Shane and Ventura.

"I think that's the point. You want to keep checking the area out there? If nothing else, it means they have to stand there like idiots, too."

They turned their backs on Ross and continued down the ridge above the canyon, following his property line until they were so far south that only his fence remained in view, pacing them to the west and with little else to speak of.

"What kind of ranch is this?" Shane asked after they had walked for fifteen minutes or more. "His land is just empty desert."

They had seen nothing else on their walk. Nothing on Ross' property, but nothing in the canyon or the desert, either. No signs of any other ghosts, and certainly no other murder victims or missing people.

"No idea. He has a barn and stables; there might be horses or something. I'll look into it."

The ridge angled down eventually, and the canyon became little more than an indentation in the rock with the same dry riverbed winding through it. It came to a stop at a rocky basin under a different cliff face, with what looked like it might have been a waterfall in another era but was now just dry, smooth stone.

"Crime scene is that way?" Shane pointed northeast.

Ventura looked at the sky and then pulled out his phone, checking his map.

"Pretty much. Few hundred yards. There's nothing out here at all."

"I noticed," Shane agreed.

If anything, there was even less than he expected. A lack of anything suspicious should not have made him suspicious, but he couldn't help himself. The handless ghost, the empty ranch with the chain-link cages, everything seemed a little off to him.

They doubled back after crossing the narrow riverbed and turned away from the ranch and toward the crime scene. It was closer than Shane expected, and the geography of the desert had played some havoc with his sense of direction. With so much nothing around him, it was hard to keep a mental map as accurate as one in a city or even a forest might have been.

Shane walked directly to the shallow graves where the two men had been discovered and stopped next to them. They were little more than faint dips in the desert sand now, filled in and smoothed over. In another day or two, only those who knew where to look would ever notice them again, and soon enough, they'd vanish entirely, swallowed by the sand.

"Little less than a mile from Ross' ranch to the highway." Shane shielded his eyes from the sun as he looked into the distance. "Ghost could be based there and reach the end of his tether just beyond the road."

Ventura pulled his phone back out and brought up the map. He put a pin in the center of the ranch house and used two fingers to expand a highlighter circle around it to a radius of one mile.

"Keeps the other bodies in range." He showed Shane the map.

"Should have the locals focus their search for the missing people in the circle, then. See what they can turn up."

"Lot of empty ground to cover, and these guys aren't exactly Columbo," Ventura said.

"How old are you?" Shane asked.

"What? Why?"

"You watch Columbo?"

"When I was a kid," Ventura answered. "My mom liked it."

"You were on a path to being a good guy even back then, huh?" Shane said.

"Weren't you?"

Shane didn't answer. Instead, he pointed to the map.

"Let's make it easier on them. Take this quadrant on the way back to the car. Looks like there are a lot of rocks and cliffs around here. Could be some good hiding places."

* * *

They started back to the north, straying from the path Ventura had used when driving to the scene. If the ghost was based on Ross' ranch, then at least they had a search grid. That was still an if, though. They could be wasting their time on assumptions, but there was little else to go on.

Ventura realized that ghosts made terrible suspects. They didn't leave many clues, they weren't susceptible to witnesses, and standard investigative techniques fell short in many cases. It wasn't like a ghost had to check in at home or work, or might get caught by a cell phone tower ping or a credit card trail.

The dead didn't need to follow the rules of the living. You couldn't stake them out or wait for them to repeat patterns of behavior. You couldn't count on anything.

Ventura didn't like not knowing what to do. He didn't like having to throw out the rule book and his instincts and rely on something more primal. Cop instincts and gut instincts weren't always the same, and right now, they were very much at odds. It was a hard thing to reconcile in his mind.

Shane Ryan made it look easy, and that frustrated him, too. It wasn't easy. He'd seen Shane almost die more than once already, and they barely knew each other. They'd worked a couple of cases together after Ventura came after him thinking he was a serial killer. Now, their fates seemed almost intertwined, and Shane had come across the country after a single phone call to help him track a murderous ghost. Those weren't cop instincts; they were something more.

"How do you know what to look for? How do you know when a ghost is going to be like Herbert and help you out or like that handless guy and try to kill you?" Ventura asked.

He had been able to see spirits since he was very young, but Shane's experience was so much different. He had tried to not see them, to not acknowledge them or let them know he was aware. They had terrified him as a child.

As an adult, he had come to accept the presence of the dead and not bring them up in front of others. He understood people thought he was crazy if he mentioned it, a lesson taken to heart when he was still a boy. To save his sanity, and his potential for a career, he kept it all to himself. Until he met Shane Ryan.

The idea that someone could fight a ghost was not something Ventura had ever imagined. It defied logic. There was nothing to touch and nothing to interact with. He had been in too many close calls over the years to think it could be different. Yet it was.

Where Ventura had been at the mercy of the dead who wanted to hurt him—some of whom very nearly succeeded—Shane Ryan could dish it all right back to them. He wanted to know more about how it worked. How Shane honed his instincts, how he knew where to go, what to do, and when to do it.

"Pretty simple," Shane answered as they trudged through the heat and sand. "You can tell a ghost has bad intentions if it tries to murder you. If it just wants to talk, that's usually a good sign."

Ventura scoffed.

"Not helpful," he replied.

Shane shrugged.

"How do you know a suspect is going to run instead of talk to you? Or what makes you draw your weapon before anyone else throws down?"

Ventura grunted. Instincts. Intuition. All the stuff he didn't think he had when it came to the dead.

"That can come with time, right?"

"I have to assume," Shane said. "Everything does."

"It's just… the locals are investigating this as a standard murder," he said.

Shane nodded.

"Cops will do that. Hell, you did that."

"But if they continue with that, that's where it would end. Unsolved murder and no suspects. Maybe there'd be more, but they'd never find the killer because they literally can never find the killer."

"One of the perks to being both dead and homicidal," Shane said. "You can get away with a lot."

"But how many other murderers are like that? Every day, how many people are being killed or going missing because of a ghost? No one's solving these crimes. No one ever will."

"Probably not," Shane agreed, "but there are a few more people like us out there who can see the dead and don't like them going off half-cocked."

"How many more?" Ventura asked.

"Not many, but some. I've met some interesting folks. You probably will too, eventually."

"Once I get over the sense of dread every time I deal with a ghost, I guess. The fear that I'm going to die."

"Nah." Shane chuckled. "We're all going to die someday, Ventura. They didn't teach you that at FBI school?"

CHAPTER 7

EYES THAT WATCH

It was early in the evening when Shane and Ventura decided it was time to head back to the city. They had covered a large swath of the quadrant Shane had pointed out on the map and discovered nothing. No sign of their homicidal ghost, no more bodies, and nothing of the missing family.

Neither man had remembered to bring bottled water or anything to protect them from the scorching sun. Ventura was already afraid that his skin was going to blister and peel, but Shane didn't care all that much. He'd been under worse sun in worse deserts.

"I'll see what we've turned up on Ross once I'm back at my hotel," Ventura said when they reached the car. "Might be something we can use. If not him, then the property itself. If Handless was as old as he seemed, maybe this all predates Ross' time on the ranch."

"Maybe," Shane agreed.

He had no plans to do much research; that was not his area of expertise. The idea of talking to some local spirits had occurred to him, but if they were anything like the ghosts in the parking lot of his hotel, he wouldn't have much luck.

He didn't think he'd be able to find any information worth his time in the city, anyway. He was letting Ventura take the lead on things. There was only so much they could do with such little information to begin with. Ventura would have to find the direction for them to head in before anything else happened.

The mystery seemed to be exciting Ventura and got him inspired about different ways to track down new leads. Shane just let him talk on the drive back into Vegas, confident that he would figure out what he needed to figure out when he needed to figure it out.

FBI procedures were not something that Shane was particularly keen on, and certainly nothing he had a background in. But Ventura sounded like he had a full plate to see him through to the next morning, so that was something.

Shane was still hung up on the handless ghost and the cages behind Ross' house. He felt like they were different pieces of a puzzle, but that the whole thing was just too big for him to see yet.

He was certain the murders had been random. He had little faith that the missing family was still alive, and he was certain the same fate had befallen them as had the ones they already found.

The timing was another puzzle piece that didn't fit anywhere that he could see yet. The ghost had been doing all its killing recently, so it was certainly not whoever had killed the handless ghost. And as Ventura had already asked, what could have set it off? Either it had only been introduced to the area just before the killing started, or it had been there for a while and was only now free.

"Check for missing people shortly before the killings started," Shane suggested. "Maybe our ghost is a victim of someone else and is doing some revenge killing. I've seen it happen before."

"Good thinking," Ventura said.

They had entered the Las Vegas city limits and were driving down the brightly lit streets while Ventura navigated toward Shane's hotel.

"Do you want to get some dinner or something?" the agent asked.

Shane raised an eyebrow and looked at the other man.

"Why'd you say it like that?"

"Like what?"

"Like it's a date."

Ventura made a face and shook his head.

"I didn't ask you on a date; I asked if you wanted dinner. You ate bacon and toast today, how are you not hungry?"

Shane pulled a cigarette from his pocket and slipped it between his lips before smiling.

"Feasting on smoke, bud. I'm good. We'll do breakfast again tomorrow, but I'll pick the restaurant. I want to get the lay of the land tonight, ask some of the dead what they've seen around town."

"You're kind of a weird guy," Ventura said. "No offense."

Shane laughed and lit the cigarette, drawing in a deep lungful before exhaling out the open window.

"Been called a lot worse," he said.

They were still on the Strip, and Shane watched drunks and revelers and police and gamblers move in a steady stream from casinos to restaurants to hotels and more. Ghosts moved unseen among them. Some looked like lost tourists; others were decayed and monstrous but weaved through crowds, unseen except by him and Ventura.

He could see how Ventura reacted when he saw something he knew was a ghost. It was subtle, very discreet, and not likely to attract attention from anyone who wasn't looking for it. The agent's eyes froze for a moment, trained on the spirit before him, and then quickly darted away.

Shane guessed that even a ghost looking at Ventura would not notice. They would regard him as they regarded any living person, see his eyes basically look through them, and have no idea that they'd been seen. This was a defense mechanism for Ventura. There were too many people in the world for most ghosts to bother harassing. But if they saw someone they knew could see them, they often focused on that person.

From what Ventura had told him in the past, Shane knew that he had dealt with spirits coming after him as a child. Growing up, he would have learned how to hide the fact that he could see them. He would have learned not to draw attention to himself so that most spirits would pass him by and not care. It was a smart thing to do, especially for someone who couldn't defend himself against an angry ghost.

The real test was with the ghosts who wanted to be seen. They were not common. Most didn't care for the living and wanted little to do with them, but some would seek out those who could see them. It was almost like fishing. All it took was throwing a scare toward someone, and if they reacted, the ghost had everything they needed. Training yourself to not react to that was hard.

"You ever talk to them?" Shane asked as they left the Strip. A legless ghost on the corner was crawling toward a restaurant while people walked through its body, barely reacting to the sudden chill they felt.

"Who?"

"Ghosts. Random ones on the street."

"No," Ventura answered. "Not if I can help it."

"Think about it. Around crime scenes, places where your suspects live, whatever. They never sleep, they listen to everything, and they know more than any witness you'll ever round up."

"But they can't testify in court, I can't list them as witnesses, and if they want to murder me, I can't defend myself," Ventura said.

"Real glass-half-empty kind of guy, are you?"

"Just being practical."

"I guess," Shane said. "But say you're looking for a killer. A regular, human one. You've got no leads, this guy is not leaving any evidence, and then you see a ghost at a crime scene, and he tells you the killer is a guy named Paul Jones who lives three doors down. Is that not helpful, even if you can't use it in court?"

"When is that ever going to happen?" Ventura pulled into the parking lot of Shane's hotel.

"Never, if you don't ask." Shane got out of the car and banged on the roof before taking a step back. "Same time tomorrow. I'll call you with a real restaurant that doesn't charge sixty bucks for toast."

"You could have eaten more than toast." Ventura put the car into reverse.

Shane watched the FBI agent go and then glanced over at the gambling ghosts in his parking lot. The dealer looked at him, a pensive expression on his face, and then returned to focus on the game.

"Where's a good place to go around here to find someone with their ear to the ground?" Shane hovered over the three spirits as they played.

"Like a dead guy?" the female ghost asked.

"MGM Grand," the dealer ghost said.

"You should stay at the Grand," the third ghost said. "Better place than this dump."

"I'd leave now if I were you," the dealer added.

"Helpful." Shane exhaled smoke. "This guy's got a pair of kings."

He pointed to the ghost in front of him and started down the street, the curses of the ghost whose hand he ruined following him.

There was too much space between the city and the murders in the desert for any of the ghosts involved to have crossed paths, but it didn't mean no one knew anything. Old ghosts had to know of the reputation that Ventura had spoken of, the history of mob hits. Maybe something linked to the handless ghost.

If not the handless spirit, then surely Ross had contacts in town. Vegas was the nearest city; he had to do his business there. Shopping, banking, any of that stuff. People knew him somewhere in town.

The Strip was all a distraction, and Shane had no interest in it. If there was anything to be found, he'd find it in the areas away from the tourism. It might have been a needle in a haystack, but ghosts liked to talk. Ventura needed to learn how to use the resources at his disposal.

The farther Shane traveled, the more spirits he saw, but most seemed to have no interest in anything around them. He spoke to one outside of a diner, and it didn't even turn to look at him. Another inside a twenty-four-hour laundromat simply faded through the wall when he asked it a question.

A pair of ghosts at the Natural History Museum were more than willing to chat with him but had nothing interesting to say. They had a nearly endless supply of stories about elderly tourists and the various mishaps they incurred on museum property, but nothing Shane could make use of.

Shane left them to discuss the things they'd seen people do in the bathroom and headed north a few more blocks until he found Woodlawn Cemetery. It was an older cemetery, and the outside looked a little scruffy with several homeless people hanging out by the gates and trash piled around the exterior fences.

He saw many spirits on the inside, most of whom were loitering the same as the homeless people on the outside, everyone just standing around and waiting for something to happen. For a city built on excitement, the population of the dead seemed entirely disengaged.

Shane saw a lot of flowers on graves, and someone put in the effort to maintain the grounds, trimming trees and mowing lawns. Some of the graves dated to the early nineteen hundreds, and Shane saw that many of the spirits were from that era based on how they were dressed.

The sun was already setting when Shane began his trek through the trees, among the tombstones, not expecting any specific information but hoping to at least learn something from someone.

Many of the Woodlawn spirits shied away, some going so far as to recede into their graves. He wondered if it was some affectation of Vegas, perhaps the result of being overwhelmed by the constant stream of tourists and unrelenting noise and lights. Shane knew firsthand how easily the dead could get frustrated and annoyed. Perhaps they had all just had enough and realized there was no way to escape it.

He found a small grave nestled between two trees with a man standing over it, leaning against one of the trees. The ghost wore a wide-brimmed hat and a dark suit, and his mouth was obscured behind a wide, thick mustache.

"You ask a lot of questions," the ghost said before Shane could speak to him.

"Can't learn anything new if you don't ask questions," Shane replied.

The ghost smiled. His face was sallow, and he had bruises across his flesh.

"Well, why don't you ask me a question or two?" he said.

"Alright, then. This you?" Shane pointed down to the grave.

The ghost nodded, and Shane read the inscription on the discrete, flat stone.

"Diamondfield. Not a common name," Shane said.

"Never was a common man," Diamondfield replied. "What do you need, friend?"

CHAPTER 8
KILLERS

Diamondfield Jack had spent more than a year on death row and survived two scheduled executions before his sentence was commuted and ultimately overturned for the murder of some shepherds in Idaho. He moved to Las Vegas, struck it rich, and was hit by a taxi in the 1940s.

"Did you kill those men?" Shane asked.

Diamondfield grinned, and his burly mustache hid most of it.

"Two other boys confessed to those murders. I was rightly set free by the honorable governor of the great state of Idaho, friend."

"That wasn't a no," Shane said.

Diamondfield laughed.

"People do what they need to do," he said. "You have to keep your eyes on the horizon."

He pointed west, and Shane looked. The sun was set now and only streaks of color peeked above the tops of buildings.

"But you don't know anything about any ghosts out in the desert?" Shane said. He'd been trying to keep Diamondfield on topic. The ghost was a little scurrilous, but maybe a little too self-interested to hold a long-term conversation.

"I died in town, friend," Diamondfield said. "But I knew some shady characters who stayed out of the lights, if you follow me. Whereabouts is your creeper doing his ill deeds?"

"Do you know the Boulder Creek Ranch?" Shane asked. Diamondfield barked a laugh.

"Pat Hendershot's ranch? In the Garvey Valley?" His grin was wider than ever.

Shane shook his head.

"Boulder Creek is all I know. Guy named Ross owns it these days," he explained.

"Well, I don't know any Ross, but as you can tell, I am not a man of the world at all these days and rarely attend social functions in and about town."

"Of course," Shane replied.

"Boulder Creek Ranch was where Pat Hendershot used to stash anything and everything he could make a buck off of. He was *the* premier moonshiner in Nevada between nineteen nineteen and nineteen twenty-three. Hendershot never met a dollar he couldn't earn in an underhanded way."

"How big was his operation?" Shane asked.

"Nevada, son," Diamondfield said. "He ran all of Nevada. Parts of Cali and Arizona, too. I'm sure he was making a mint. Tight-lipped fella, mind you. Not prone to sharing his secrets."

"But shared enough for you to know he was a moonshiner," Shane said. Diamondfield shrugged.

"I wasn't always a man of integrity, and our darker instincts might have seen us run among the same lower-class circles from time to time."

"From time to time," Shane said with a nod. Diamondfield kept smiling.

"Yes, sir. I can see it in your eyes that you are a man after my own heart. Maybe inclined to eschew the odd unlawful order in pursuit of your own greater good, am I correct?"

Shane had to laugh at the man's choice of words.

"I've been known to run in lower-class circles from time to time, Diamondfield. And right now, that's taking me back to that ranch. I checked out the property, and there's a barn but not much else. Even if the man was moonshining in the present, it's a bit of a stretch to get to murder by ghost."

"Of course, of course," Diamondfield said. "But the desert out that way is full of secrets if you know where to look. Canyons, caves, and old gold and silver mines. They're everywhere, and I can tell you that not every man who went out to find riches came home again. Wouldn't be surprised at all to find the ghost of a fortune-seeker thereabouts."

The cemetery was fully dark now, and many of the other spirits wandered lazily about the grounds. Shane heard people outside the gates. Pedestrians, the homeless camped out front, and others were going about their business with no idea what was happening a few feet away. Neither the living nor the dead seemed to care about one another.

"Seems like I need to take a closer look at some of those canyons," Shane said.

"Couldn't hurt. Unless, of course, someone kills you," Diamondfield warned.

"Thanks for your time."

Shane extended a hand, and the ghost laughed again. He took Shane's hand aggressively, as though expecting to swipe through him, and grunted when his palm made contact with Shane's.

"Well, I'll be damned," Diamondfield said.

"Maybe," Shane replied. "Take care."

Shane left the cemetery and headed back toward his hotel. The streets were not much different at night than they were during the day. The ghosts of Vegas did not seem to care about the time of day. Maybe it was because the city never got dark with all the flashing lights. The dead couldn't hide in the dark in Las Vegas the way they could in other cities. Not downtown, anyway.

Back at the hotel, Shane was surprised to see that the gamblers from the parking lot were gone. He had come to think they were permanent fixtures, but their absence meant they found other things to do with their time now and then.

In place of the ghosts, there were a couple of new cars in the lot that indicated some other desperate souls had selected the out-of-the-way rundown hotel as their destination. Most people heading to Las Vegas to gamble probably wouldn't have cared if they stayed in a cardboard box, which was arguably the best-selling point for a hotel like that.

Shane headed to his room at the top of one of the hotel's little towers. The stairway was hot on the way up, with the lack of air conditioning in the building extremely noticeable at night when the outside was cooler than the inside.

The hallways smelled strange, with the heat bringing up odors emanating from the rooms. Shane approached his room, not minding the muffled sounds of other people's televisions and an argument on the floor below penetrating the walls. He didn't have much to go on in terms of information and felt no need to get in touch with Ventura. The idea that there might be caves or old mines to search was not groundbreaking. He'd wait until morning and see what the FBI agent could dig up.

Ventura had to have better resources to rely on than a few disinterested ghosts with memories from a half-century ago. If there was something to be found about Bennet Ross or the land, he'd find it. If all else failed, he could lean into the search warrant and get them onto the property to look for evidence.

Shane entered his room and shut the door behind him. The curtains were still drawn, and the room was black. Normally, he would have locked the door and hit the light switch, but he didn't this time.

The heat of the room was close to stifling and brought musty odors from the carpet and bathroom, something he'd noticed the day before. But there was a new smell in the room, some kind of fragrant aftershave, or maybe just deodorant working overtime in the heat. It was the smell of another person.

He was on the floor before the door latch finished clicking. The sound of splintering wood coincided with a sharp, metallic click. Shane recognized the noise in the dark without needing to see it. Muffled though it might have been, it was a gunshot suppressed by a silencer. Not so quiet as the movies made it seem, but quiet enough that anyone nearby would think it was just the pipes or someone banging on a wall.

Shane moved swiftly, half-crouched as he scrambled into the room toward the source of the noise. His assailant would have had to adjust to the sudden light of him opening the door, so his window to act was short.

His eyes adjusted quickly, the curtains only keeping out so much light, and he saw the man standing in the bathroom doorway and lowering the weapon with his eyes locked on Shane to fire a second round.

Shane grabbed the weapon and took out the man's legs, forcing him to the ground as he tossed the gun aside. It was hard to make out in the dark, but something was vaguely familiar about the man. He had been at Ross' ranch. One of the other men with him in the back, watching Shane and Ventura on the ridge.

The gun skittered across the floor, and Shane slammed an elbow into the man's face, feeling bone and cartilage crunch even as the man bit off a cry of pain. He reached out blindly, grabbing hold of the nightstand drawer, pulling it out, and swinging it down on top of the man's head.

The cheap wood shattered, and Shane hit the man again with the plank of wood still adorned with the handle. His attacker shifted his weight and disarmed Shane, punching him in the kidney several times as they wrestled across the floor in the dark.

Shane could not see the gun, but he couldn't risk the other man getting a hold of it. He kept up the attack, driving a knee into the other man's groin and pushing his elbow down on his throat. Neither of them said anything, only exchanging groans of pain and grunts of effort as each tried to get the upper hand.

The other man was strong and handled himself well enough. He quickly adapted to Shane's attacks and countered with smart, efficient moves. There was some stiffness in this movement, though. Shane guessed that, while he was proficient, he didn't fight regularly. At least not recently.

Whoever he was, and however he had been trained, Shane didn't want him to find his legs again. If he got into a rhythm, gained some more confidence, and got the upper hand, Shane didn't doubt the man would kill him.

The other man stood, and Shane moved with him, seizing the opportunity to get on his feet again as well. They didn't let one another go, and Shane drove several sharp punches into the man's gut and another into his chin before they were both upright.

The attacker went for Shane's face, swinging with a right hook but timing it all wrong as Shane drove his shoulder into the man's stomach, knocking him across the bed. Shane followed quickly, lifting the man as he fell and then slamming him hard against the window through the curtains. The glass broke with a dull crunch, insulated by the thick curtains, and fragments fell to the floor.

Shane flinched as the man came for his face again, not with punches this time but with his fingers extended like claws. He tried to drive a thumb into Shane's eyes but couldn't follow through as Shane wrapped the curtain around the attacker's head, pulling it tight once he was fully ensconced.

The stranger struggled against the thick fabric, abandoning his attack to pull the material away from his throat. Shane twisted a handful of the dark, synthetic weave, choking the other man while the curtain covered his face like a hood.

As Shane increased the pressure on the twisted fabric, the gunman kicked out violently, just missing Shane's groin and clipping his thigh instead. The force of the blow knocked Shane back to the bed but forced the man back into the broken window.

With the glass missing, there was nothing to stop the attacker's momentum. He tumbled back through the broken glass, dragging the curtains with him as he fell.

Shane rushed to the window as the lights of the parking lot filled his room. The gunman landed with a dull thud in the lot below, the curtain around his head absorbing most of the sound.

For a moment, Shane was certain the man had died, but the body twitched and he slowly reached up a hand to pull the curtain from his face.

"Seriously?" Shane said quietly.

He left the room and headed downstairs. He still hadn't gotten a good look at the man's face, but he was certain he was Ross' man. Shane hadn't gotten a clear look at the man's face at the ranch either, but if he was still alive, Shane would get him to talk.

The neighborhood was deader than the missing parking lot gamblers. No one had seen the attacker fall from the window or, if they had, they hadn't wanted to get involved. There wasn't even a scream from a witness. People in Vegas were wrapped up in their own thing.

Shane reached the man's side, and he had already pulled the curtain away from his face. Blood ran from his nose and his mouth, and his eyes were scrunched shut while he breathed in a loud, labored manner.

"You look like hell," Shane said.

The man's eyes fluttered open, and another muffled shot rang out. Blood sprayed across the parking lot as bone and flesh burst from the man's temple.

Shane ducked quickly behind a soda machine, scanning the road. He saw no sign of a second gunman, no moving cars, no people in windows across the street, nothing. The shot had been perfect. It blew off the entire right side of the man's head, and there was no doubt now that he was dead.

CHAPTER 9
BENDING AND BREAKING

Shane lit another cigarette and leaned against the soda machine. The police officer in the parking lot kept staring at him while talking to a second officer. Occasionally, he stared back and offered a wave if somebody new joined their conversation.

The body of the would-be assassin was covered but had yet to be moved. Shane had given a statement when the police arrived, and they had already asked him to clarify it twice.

"He was waiting in your room? To rob you?"

"I never asked what he wanted. He tried to shoot me."

"Did he follow you from a casino, maybe? Are you carrying a lot of cash on you?"

"He was waiting. He didn't follow me."

"But you did win a lot of money somewhere?"

The idea that a man had been waiting to shoot him and was not robbing him of his imaginary casino winnings was apparently hard for the Las Vegas Police to understand.

"And you've never seen him before?"

"Never," Shane said.

"Have you received any threats lately?"

"I've been in Vegas for a day. No."

Someone had gone to find hotel security tapes. There were a handful of cameras around, and they were functional, which surprised Shane. At best, they would show the police when the man showed up, and then confirm the rest of his story. Not that there was much to tell beyond what he'd already said.

"Why did you come down to the parking lot after the victim fell out of the window?"

"Because he was waiting in my room to kill me, and I wanted to know why," Shane answered.

"You didn't think to call the police right away?"

"Why? Do you know why he wanted to kill me?"

They didn't seem to be great fans of his answers, but at least they hadn't decided he was a murderer right off the bat. The security footage likely showed that the man had preceded Shane, they had found his gun, and everything so far looked like a case of self-defense.

By the time Ventura showed up, there were detectives on site ready to ask Shane the same questions a third time. Ventura flashed his badge to get past everyone and joined Shane at the soda machine.

"One day, and you already killed a guy?" he said.

"He started it," Shane explained. "Shot at me in my room."

"You just draw in chaos like a magnet," Ventura said.

He approached the dead man's body and crouched. Forensics were still in Shane's room pulling the slug from his door and looking for anything else the dead man had left behind. Some of his hotel neighbors had come out to watch. A few had tried to check out but were detained until the police could question them.

Ventura waved Shane over and lowered his voice.

"You recognize this guy?"

"Thought he might have been at Ross' ranch. We didn't have a long time to get to know each other."

"Yeah, well, I already know him," the agent said. "Guy's from Philly. His name's Nic Canterino. Used to go by Lobo, but no one ever called him that for real. Little Nicky was the name that stuck. He's a made guy."

"Like the mob?" Shane asked.

"The mob," Ventura confirmed.

Shane chuckled, and Ventura shot him a stern look.

"What the hell are you laughing at?"

"The mob. The mafia? Like Goodfellas?"

"Call it organized crime if you prefer, but these guys are still running rackets. Extortion, murder, gambling, fraud; it's a wide-reaching deal, and it's serious."

"So, what's he doing in Las Vegas trying to shoot me in a crappy hotel?"

"That, I don't know," Ventura said. "This is way out of left field."

"Do these guys even run anything in Vegas anymore?"

Ventura stood, leading Shane away from the corpse and the cops.

"Yes and no. The casino business isn't theirs anymore, but you can't get organized crime out of any city. Strip clubs, prostitution, loan sharking, that sort of thing is still linked to some families."

"Including these guys in Philly?"

Ventura shook his head. He didn't know.

"Was this one of the guys on Ross' ranch? I didn't get the best look at the other two he was hanging out with, but that was my first guess when I was getting this guy's fist in my kidney on the floor of my room."

Ventura looked back at the body and ran a hand through his hair, holding it at the back of his head and scratching for a moment.

"Think it was, but I wouldn't testify to it. I know that doesn't mean much to you, but yeah. I'm not ready to go in guns blazing on a half-recognized face."

"For what it's worth, I got word that the area around the ranch has a history of unscrupulous activity. Bootlegging, that sort of thing. And there are probably some caves and mines in the area from back in the day that have seen their fair share of blood."

"You got that from him?" Ventura referred to the body.

"No, a ghost. Said the place is a bit infamous, but that was seventy years ago."

"Seventy? Jesus, Ryan."

"Caves are caves; doesn't matter how long ago we're talking. What I'm saying is that we might not be seeing everything on the surface. You might want to put a rush on that warrant."

Regardless of what they might find, it was clear the man who tried to kill Shane was somehow tied to the ranch. Shane hadn't been anywhere else since he'd gotten to Las Vegas, and no one else had seen his face or knew anything about him. Ross had jumped the gun and tipped his hand too soon by sending someone after Shane.

Ventura glanced at the nearby police officers and then lowered his voice, keeping his eyes off Shane as he looked around the parking lot.

"There's not going to be a warrant," he said.

It was clear he was trying to be discreet without looking like he was trying to be discreet. Shane took another puff of his cigarette and exhaled to one side.

"Meaning?" he said.

"I'm not working in Vegas right now. None of this is sanctioned or on the books."

Shane tried not to laugh. Ventura was stressed out by even admitting that to Shane, but Shane found it endlessly amusing that Ventura might be breaking some rules.

"You're going to have to explain that a little further," Shane said.

Ventura grunted, glancing at him, and then looking away again.

"I came out here to relax. Got tickets to see Penn and Teller and a couple concerts. It was suggested to me that I take some time off."

Shane nodded, pulling the cigarette from his lips while watching the police discuss the crime scene.

"Boss has a beef with you?"

"I've been on thin ice for a little while. One case with inconsistencies is not a big deal. But I've got the serial killer case that led me to you, I've got Burkitt, I've got the children's hospital, I've got New York... it all came home to roost. Too many holes, and too many questions. The only reason I haven't been fired is because there's no logical explanation for the inconsistencies. The reality is ghosts, and no one is ready to accept that."

"Damn. Thought you smoothed all that out," Shane said. It seemed like Ventura was managing his work well despite the supernatural elements. Apparently, he was just good at sounding confident.

"There's more to it than that. Someone's had my back a few times. Reports had details added after the fact that accounted for missing time, property destruction, and unexplained phenomena. Someone is watching out, but at the end of the day, my director needed me gone for a while. None of this was supposed to happen."

"What if they find out you're working a case out here?" Shane asked.

"They won't. I'll say I heard about it by coincidence, which I did, and offered to help local law enforcement. Nothing else beyond that. I'm not requesting resources or sanctioning anything in the name of the bureau. It should fly under the radar, as long as I don't draw attention. Like by requesting a warrant to search a ranch."

"So that's why you called me," Shane said. "Off-the-record assistance."

"And you're better help than a dozen agents who have no idea that ghosts exist."

Shane chuckled and shrugged.

"Always knew I was better than the cops," he said.

"Yeah, that's mostly what I mean," Ventura agreed.

"Didn't you just solve the greatest serial killing crime in American history with Mr. Shadow? Isn't that worth some leeway at work?"

"Yeah, that's why I'm on vacation and not unemployed. If a firefighter is first at the scene of every fire, he's either a hero or an arsonist, that's how they're looking at me now."

"So, we've got no resources to get this done. And you wanted me to play by the book?"

"I can't break the law, even if I'm not officially working," Ventura pointed out. "I can't just break into the ranch because we think he's up to something."

"Yeah, but you keep saying 'we', for some reason. I can do that," Shane said.

"No, you can't. Breaking the law is just as illegal when you do it."

"It's only illegal if I get caught," Shane corrected.

Ventura shook his head, and Shane laughed again. One of the police officers looked over at him, and he stifled his enjoyment.

"So, what was the straw that broke the camel's back?" Shane asked. "How'd you get railroaded?"

"Burkitt," Ventura answered.

The town in Delaware was the truest ghost town Shane had seen. No one was alive there, but a ghost had been running the show for generations and killing anyone who came upon the place. Ventura had helped Shane destroy the spirit and free several ghosts under the control of an ancient spirit. But doing so had required him to keep state police and others out of the city limits until Shane's work was done.

"What did you tell them happened? Chemical spill?" Shane asked. He needed some excuse to keep people away that wouldn't be questioned. "Biological weapon?"

"Yeah, that's what came back to bite me. My conclusions were not sound, and no evidence backed up my position that prevented the potential rescue of the missing family."

"But we rescued the missing family," Shane said.

"Except for the dad," Ventura said. "They put that on me. And the numerous dead bodies we dragged out of that town after the fact."

"Those people had been dead for decades," Shane said. Everyone from Burkitt had left years before or died. There was nothing else.

"But I can't tell anyone the true story, so it makes me look incompetent at best or compromised at worst. The fact that a man died was something my director couldn't overlook, especially since I couldn't back up my reasons for keeping the rest of the bureau and the Staties out of town. By the time I got wrapped up with Beatrix and the Harvesters, it was too late. I had to leave."

"But you have a guardian angel over there somewhere, though?" Shane asked.

"Someone higher up the food chain than me. But they're staying in the shadows, and they can't work miracles."

"Mulder and Scully over here," Shane said. "Interesting times."

"Everyone thought Mulder was crazy, and no one wanted him around."

"None of us is perfect."

"No," Ventura said. "I'm not planning to end this; I wouldn't have called you here otherwise. I'm just saying, we're going to have to lean more toward your style of investigation than mine this time. Within reason."

"Oh, always," Shane said. "I plan to be very reasonable."

"I'm serious, Ryan. I could lose my job if this goes sideways. And that means you'll be back on the bureau's radar. If this goes tits up and you're brought in with me, after being involved in New York, Burkitt, the hospital, the serial killer investigation, and now this, things are going to be bad."

"Then we stay off the radar. But you have to be okay with bending the occasional law, or at least turning your head to look the other way. This won't work otherwise," Shane told him.

"I can do that," Ventura said.

Shane nodded and then gestured to the dead man on the ground.

"Then we need to head back to the ranch. I imagine that whoever shot him is going to come back to take another shot at me. And your name is probably next on the list."

"Yeah," Ventura agreed. "Just let me clear this up with the locals."

"Unofficially," Shane said.

72

"Unofficially," Ventura repeated.

CHAPTER 10

CAGED

Shane made one last official statement and Ventura assured one of the detectives that he would be back later if they needed him. They left together in Ventura's car and took a circuitous route through the Vegas streets in case anyone was still following Shane.

When they were confident no one was on their tail, they headed out of town. Ventura chose back roads through the desert rather than the direct route to the ranch. They didn't want to approach the place from the front, anyway. The plan this time was to approach from the rear and stay away from CCTV cameras. It was dark, and Shane guessed that Ross would not be expecting them to show up on his doorstep, or his back door in this case, so soon after the attack.

From what they had seen on the first day, Ross' land covered many acres, but all the buildings were tightly packed near the ranch. The rest of the land was open scrub and desert. If they could get back there and sneak closer to the barn and the main house, they might find something linking the man to the killer ghost. Failing that, Shane was on the lookout for any caves or mines that might exist on the property.

Ventura steered clear of the ranch and the road leading up to it. Instead, he took his car offroad more than a mile from the property, traveling through the desert toward the ranch on the western side.

The sky was overcast, and with no moonlight, they were all but invisible as they drove. Ventura kept the headlights off, keeping the speed down and carefully navigating around rocks and cacti. By the time the fence line for Ross' property was in view, they were well away from the main house or the road. No one would have seen them or knew where they were.

"So how much are we bending the law here?" Shane asked.

"Don't ask me that. Just go." Ventura left the car behind and followed Shane through the darkness.

There were no cameras this far from the house. The fence was just a property marker and something to keep trespassers and maybe wildlife away. Shane hopped the fence easily, boosting himself on a boulder, and Ventura came after him. They stayed low to the ground and ran along the fence up the property toward the main house.

After several minutes of navigating the dark and empty desert, a dim light grew in the distance. They angled toward it, moving quickly but quietly until they were close enough to make out what it was.

Shane saw the stables to the east and some sheds and other outbuildings to the west. The source of the light was in the middle. The cages that they had seen earlier in the day, fenced-in corrals that seemed to have no purpose, were no longer empty. Each of them held at least several dozen ghosts. The three pens sat side by side, fully loaded with spirits emanating a soft, white glow.

"There's got to be a hundred of them." Ventura crouched low to the ground.

"Looks like a graveyard, only without the graves," Shane said.

The spirits were held in by the fencing and milled about like cattle inside. Ross was running some sort of free-range ghost ranch, holding them with iron fencing so they could not escape.

The logistics and purpose were lost on Shane. No obvious haunted items were around, and with no actual graves, it was hard to understand what kept the ghosts in place. As for why, that was a whole different problem.

People collected ghosts for any number of reasons. They could be sold, used for work both legitimate and dangerous, or held just for clout.

Collectors had a dozen reasons for wanting spirits that ranged from as mundane as wanting a chess opponent to as evil as wanting an unstoppable murderer. Ross seemed like the kind of man who might not care what someone wanted the ghost for, but he had a surplus.

"You think he's selling?" Ventura asked.

"Has to be. Private collection would be kept inside and treated with more care," Shane said. "This has to be stock."

"Like a Harvesters thing? Cult of the Endless Night?"

"All of the above and more. It's a strange setup, though. Why let them roam at all?"

"You asking me?" Ventura said.

"Thinking out loud," Shane replied. "If something doesn't make sense, the reason is usually not a good one."

"Not good how?"

"Insane or horrifying, usually."

"Of course," Ventura said. "What do we do?"

"I say we go ask some questions."

Ventura looked at him unsurely.

"Someone tried to kill you just now, most probably from this ranch. I don't know if exposing ourselves is the best idea," he said.

"You have a better one? They can't come to us."

"Not really. It feels off, though. Like we're being set up. All these ghosts just out in the open where anyone can see them?"

Shane scoffed.

"No one can see them. Just you and me. Everyone else sees empty cages."

"Right." Ventura nodded.

It was easy to forget, when you got wrapped up in a haunting or another ghostly happening, that most people would never see what you did or know what you know.

Shane didn't wait for Ventura to make up his mind and started toward the cages, moving swiftly across the sand and rocks. Ventura was only a step behind, and the closer they got, the more Shane could make out the faces of the spirits in the cages.

There seemed to be very little linking the ghosts. They had clearly died from different causes at different times. Some deaths had been violent and bloody; others had left no marks. Some of the spirits looked as though they could have just died that week; others looked to be from a different century.

Movement outside one of the cages caused Shane to flatten himself into a slight dip in the ground. Ventura was at his side, watching a shape on the far side of the nearest cage walk around the outside. It was difficult to make out through the throngs of ghosts in the way, but Shane was certain it was another ghost, uncaged and seemingly on patrol around the fences.

"That's Mario Langella," Ventura whispered, pointing to the middle cage.

Shane could not tell who the agent was referring to, not that it mattered.

"He was with the Chicago mafia. Used to work for Joey Doves. He worked at the Stardust, left work to head home one night, was never seen again."

"When was that?" Shane asked.

"Seventy-one, maybe? Seventy-two?"

"And you recognize this guy in a cage full of other ghosts?"

"Look at his nose. The man had a distinct face. I used to read about the mob in Vegas for fun. It's always been an interest," Ventura explained.

"Hell of a hobby," Shane said. "So that's a dead mobster. That guy over there looks like a prospector."

He pointed out a ghost in clothes from the early nineteen hundreds at the latest. His scruffy beard was stained with blood that ran down the front of a dirty shirt and suspenders. Something had sliced his throat and bled him out.

"Looks like," Ventura agreed.

"If your Chicago mobster got dumped in the desert and this guy got shanked at a mine, then I'm thinking Ross is collecting anything he finds in the desert. He's picking up strays."

The ghost that was uncaged continued wandering around the fences. There seemed to be no pattern to where it went. Sometimes, it stopped and turned around and headed back the way it had come. It focused so much on the far side of the cages that Shane still hadn't gotten a good look at it. It seemed to be minding its own business, however, and that meant Shane and Ventura had an opening on the near side.

Shane got up again, crouching as he ran toward the edge of the fence, keeping his eye open for the cameras. From what he had seen, most of them had been angled out to monitor people breaking in, and nothing was pointed toward the cage. That made sense since none of the ghosts would have shown up on camera, anyway.

The ghosts inside the cage saw him coming, and most turned their backs immediately, walking away into the crowd.

"Hey," Shane said to the nearest spirit. "What the hell is going on here?"

The ghost ignored him, as did all the others. Shane headed toward the next cage and the ghost that Ventura had pointed out.

"Langella," he said.

The spirit looked at him and scowled. Some of the others looked at Langella, their expressions grim.

"That's you, right? Mario Langella?"

The ghost bared his teeth and came toward the fence, walking stiffly while looking over his shoulder.

"Get the hell out of here," he hissed.

Shane glanced at Ventura and then leaned in closer to the fence.

"I'm just looking for some information about this place. Why's Ross got you all corralled in here?"

"What are you, hard of hearing? I said take off," Langella's voice was a little louder this time.

More of the caged ghosts were looking at him now. They whispered among themselves, and Langella was growing nervous.

"What does he have on you?" Ventura asked.

Langella turned to the agent and scoffed.

"Look at this guy. What are you, an FBI agent?"

Shane held back his laughter as the ghost got as close to the fence as he could without touching it.

"He doesn't have 'something' on me, Bozo. He has me. He has all of us, and you're gonna get me tossed in a goddamn box. Now take off, both of you."

Langella turned away from them like a petulant child, just standing with his back to both men and refusing to speak anymore. Shane looked at the other spirits in the cage, and those in the neighboring cages, and they all averted their eyes immediately.

"So, it's a prison, and they get thrown in the hole for breaking rules," Ventura said.

It was as accurate a description as anything. Ross must have had the haunted items stashed close at hand so he could seal them up if someone got out of line. To keep them inside the cage, the items had to be underneath it.

The loose ghost made his way around the edge of the nearest cage. He stopped when he saw Shane and Ventura, one good eye locked on them while the other, badly swollen and reddish black, could focus on nothing.

The ghost was very badly burned. Burned skin and fat had fused with his clothing across his chest and shoulders, creating a mixture that oozed blood and a clear, yellow fluid.

Half of the ghost's face had been lost to the burn. All the features had melted away so badly that muscle and bone were exposed. Shane saw the ghost's teeth through a hole burned in his cheek that spread open as his jaw parted so he could produce a gurgling cry of alarm.

CHAPTER 11

PURSUIT

The ghost turned on his heels and bolted toward the farmhouse at the head of the ranch, and Shane gave chase. If the ghost was going to rat them out, and Ross had sent the assassin to kill Shane at his hotel, then they were dead the minute the ghost raised the alarm. There was no way they'd be able to get off Ross' property in time.

Thanks to the severe burns that covered half of the ghost's body, he had not died in a way that made him particularly limber. The ghost's left leg did not stretch properly, so he limped as he ran.

Shane caught up quickly and tackled the spirit just beyond the far edge of the cage. The ghost made angry sounds of protest, but none of them came close to words. If he was meant to be a guard, he would not have been very good at his job thanks to his inability to speak, but that wouldn't matter for long.

The ghost went for Shane's throat, growling and scratching like an animal. Shane pinned the ghost's hands and shifted his weight, forcing the ghost to roll over face-down into the sand.

"Settle down or I'll rip your arms off," he warned the spirit.

The ghost would not relent and tried to wrestle free. Shane forced him to calm down while Ventura crouched far enough away that the ghost could not reach him and watched for any sign of movement from the house.

"We're in range of cameras," the agent pointed out. "We need to go."

"He's not going to let us," Shane said of the ghost pinned beneath him.

It continued to squirm and buck to get free. Only one option was available.

Shane released the ghost's arms and focused on his head. He scrambled and clawed at the dirt to pull free and get to the house, but Shane ignored it. Instead, he pushed down on the back of the ghost's skull, forcing his burned face into the sand.

The ghost's flesh felt cold and not solid. The burn reminded Shane of thick peanut butter, and it oozed beneath his fingers as he added pressure. Bone cracked, and then the skull crunched, collapsing in on itself.

Ventura winced and raised an arm to shield himself as the ghost's body exploded and Shane was knocked backward into the dirt. The percussive sound was muffled somewhat by the desert sands. Wherever the ghost's haunted item was being held, there was no sign of its destruction anywhere in the yard that Shane could see.

"Do you think someone heard that?" Ventura helped Shane to his feet.

The caged ghosts had gone silent. They stared at Shane in open awe, some with outright terror on their faces after seeing what he could do. None made a sound, and the desert night was as silent as the grave it appeared to be.

"If their items are around here, then yeah, I think someone heard that," Shane said.

There was no sound from the ranch house, and no obvious movement yet. Lights were on in various windows, but they had been the entire time. Shane glanced at the nearest security camera pointed in his direction. If Ross didn't know they were there yet, he would soon enough.

"We should go," Shane said.

"Great." Ventura turned away from the house.

Things were not going the way Shane had intended. He had hoped to have at least reached the house and looked around before they had to leave the property. As it was, Ross probably had security footage of them trespassing, Shane having some sort of a fit on the ground, and then both men running away. Things were going to look bad for Ventura if word got back to the FBI that he was spending his vacation breaking and entering.

They needed to find something more concrete than a cage full of spirits. But if they didn't leave the property, little was stopping Ross from unleashing all those spirits to go after them, not to mention whatever living assassins he might have had on hand. They had bungled their recon and needed to regroup and come up with a better plan.

Nothing pursued them as they fled across the desert toward the fence line in the west. Neither ghosts nor gunshots were on their heels. It was possible that no one inside had noticed the destruction of the ghost that Shane had taken out. Still, they couldn't take the risk by continuing toward the house in the hopes of finding something to incriminate Ross.

They returned to Ventura's car, and there was still no sign of a pursuit. Shane was not convinced they were in the clear. Someone had found his hotel after their first visit, and he hadn't noticed anyone following them that time, either.

"Any one of those ghosts could have been our killer," Ventura pointed out as he drove through the desert back to the road.

"Maybe," Shane said. "I don't think he's caged, though."

"What about the one you destroyed?"

"Definitely not," Shane said. "The killer wouldn't run from a fight and let himself get destroyed that easily."

"He's got to be connected to Ross, though," Ventura said.

He wasn't wrong. Shane didn't doubt there was a connection, but it was not an obvious one. The ghosts in the cages, even Ventura's mobster, were subdued and beaten down. It was a prison, as he had said. They were being held and controlled. The ghost that was killing didn't appear to be under control.

Shane had originally thought he might be a pet or something Ross was sending out, but that didn't make sense to him now. Ross liked to be in control. The guard ghost hadn't spared a moment's thought before running to the ranch. Shane was positive it was just an extra layer of protection, like the cameras. Ross liked to see and know everything. The killer ghost was outside of his control; it had to be. Killing random travelers and leaving the bodies where they could be found was not neat and tidy.

"Maybe something Ross lost," Shane suggested.

The logistics still didn't make sense. If Ross had the ghost's haunted item, he could box it up, like Langella said. Ross did not have the killer's item, but it was still in the area, and that was just too much of a coincidence for it not to be connected.

The ghost in the canyon came to mind then. That spirit's haunted item—his body—had been in the rocks. He was close to Ross, and close to the ranch, but free. Maybe the killer was like that.

Shane was still missing something. He needed to know more. He needed to see the ghost, find out who it was or why it was killing. There were too many variables. Organized crime ties with the hitman, the ranch's history of bootlegging, the deaths, and the cages. Lots of little pieces that did not connect to see the big picture.

The car was back on the road as Ventura drove them away from the ranch and back toward the city. Shane checked the mirror several times but saw no one in obvious pursuit. Still, the nagging suspicion followed him that they were not out of the woods.

"Where are we headed?" He looked in the mirror.

The road behind them was dark, but he felt like something was hidden in the shadows. A car with the lights off, too far behind to be seen. Every so often, he thought he caught a glimpse of something, a quick reflection off something metal, but it was so fast and so distant that he couldn't be sure. Maybe it was just the paranoia of having almost been shot earlier.

"Where do you want to go?" Ventura asked.

"If Ross had sent the gunman, chances are he knows your hotel just as he knew mine. We need to get lost."

"Where?"

"Where is the best place to fade into a crowd?"

Ventura laughed.

"It's Vegas. You can do that in a hundred places."

"Pick the biggest one," Shane said.

Ventura nodded, taking a right toward the lights of Las Vegas.

"I'd take you back to the Wynn, but I don't want you to panic over the buffet again. We'll go to the MGM Grand. Should be more than enough to lose someone. About seventy thousand people go through the doors every day. If there is anyone to lose, we'll lose them."

He looked in the rearview while Shane kept an eye on the side mirror.

"You see that?" Ventura said after a moment.

Shane had seen a glint, far behind and lost in blackness. But if Ventura had seen it too, it was something.

"Yeah," he replied.

"Okay," Ventura said. "MGM Grand it is."

Shane had never spent any real time in Las Vegas. The big casinos, the big crowds, the lights, and the noise were all things that were the opposite of what appealed to him in terms of a vacation. Different strokes for different folks were one thing, but losing your life savings on a slot machine while you ate sixty-dollar toast wasn't his cup of tea.

The massive crowds and noise were perfect urban camouflage, though. No one could track them through a casino that saw the population of some smaller cities wander its floors daily.

By the time they were back in the city, too many cars were turning off side streets and pulling out of parking lots to track anyone who might have followed them from out of town. Shane gave up on watching the mirrors and focused on the road ahead.

Lights on both sides of the road were all but blinding. Las Vegas at night was a grand testament to wasted electricity and excess. Anything that could be used to grab someone's attention was deployed at the highest level. It was sensory overload, nonstop from every direction.

He saw ghosts moving among the crowds of pedestrians and revelers. There were not many of them, and those that were out with the living looked to be having as good a time as everyone else. Shane rarely saw happy ghosts on the streets, smiling and even laughing, but that was what was happening. At least someone was enjoying Vegas and everything it offered.

The MGM Grand looked like a science fiction monster as they approached. Green lights against black glass with yellow signage made it look like an alien fortress. Shane knew it would be big based on what Ventura had said, but he had not expected it to look like a city block.

They pulled up to a valet stand and Ventura handed over his keys before they headed into the casino. So much of everything was going on that Shane was surprised people willingly stayed there. From psychedelic carpeting to the endless clanging and ringing of slot machines, it was like a dozen fever dreams crashed together in one place.

Ventura led them swiftly away from the door, across the floor, and around a bank of slot machines to the lobby bar. The small, round room was raised on a dais and offered a nearly three-sixty view of the casino near the doors. They took a table and sat, looking for familiar faces.

"You hungry?" the agent asked after they ordered drinks. "We could order sliders."

Shane kept his eyes on the ever-moving crowd.

"Knock yourself out." Shane was more interested in waiting to see who showed up than snacks. But Ventura was on vacation, he supposed.

CHAPTER 12

WHAT'S IN THE DARK

Bennett Ross was not known for his patience. He understood it was a character flaw, and he had worked on it in the past. Even when he was a kid, he got out of bed just after midnight on Christmas and opened his presents before his parents or his siblings were awake. It got so bad that his parents wouldn't put the gifts out until they were up the next morning.

His bad habit of jumping the gun had backfired, he knew that. He shouldn't have sent Canterino into the city to go after the FBI agent and his partner. Now he was dead, tossed out of a window in a sleazebag hotel.

That the two men stayed at different hotels had confused Ross. The bald guy was not FBI, and Ross had no idea who he was. The other one, Agent Ventura, was also perplexing. As far as Ross could tell, the FBI was not working a case in town.

The desert deaths had been linked. State Police were investigating them as one crime, including the missing persons. They were probably a few days away from a press conference when the term "serial killer" would be tossed out, and then there would be too many eyes on the ranch and the desert around it.

If there was one thing Ross didn't like, it was unnecessary attention. He didn't like people coming to the ranch, and he didn't like people asking questions. He didn't like people much at all, to be honest. Everything was going to pot, and it annoyed him something fierce.

"I just don't understand why you didn't shoot the bald guy when you had the chance. Why the hell did you shoot Nic?"

"Law enforcement would have snatched him if he was still alive,"

Barclay answered.

Dennis Barclay sounded smarter than he was. It was the accent. The Brit had been in the U.S. for several years, but his accent gave him an air of sophistication. Ross had worked with the man long enough to know it was an illusion. Barclay was an accomplished killer, good with a gun and good at tracking down a target, but not the best thinker to play the game.

"You should have shot them both."

"The bald guy took cover. Police were on the way."

Ross sighed. He didn't want to explain why the other man could have killed the target first and then followed up with Canterino if there was any worry about him spilling to the cops. There was no changing the past.

"And now you've lost them," Ross said.

"Yes, sir," Barclay admitted. "I had them until somewhere around Caesar's Palace, but they disappeared in traffic."

"They didn't go back to this Ventura's hotel?"

"No, sir," Barclay replied. "I assume they've abandoned those rooms."

"After the failed attempt to kill him in his hotel? Yes, Dennis, I think that's a reasonable assumption."

Ventura and his partner had been on the property just after the failed hit. They must have come right to the ranch after Canterino flew out the window. If Ross had been a little more patient, maybe waited another day or two, the link between himself and Canterino wouldn't have been as strong. Not that it would have mattered if the man had done the job properly, but that was spilled milk.

The men knew that Ross had put a hit on them and had returned to the ranch, arguably to hold him to account. But it had just been the two of them; there was no police backup. More concerning was that they saw the cages.

"These two are not working an active case. This is off the books," Ross said.

"Yes, sir. My contacts confirmed Ventura is on leave with the bureau. He's supposed to be here on vacation."

"Find them. Use whoever you need to in town. Find out who the bald man is and what they're doing here. Then kill them," Ross instructed.

"Yes, sir," Barclay replied.

He left the room without another word, heading back out of the house to return to the city. Ross waited until he heard the other man's car pulling off the property before he went deeper into the house.

Ross unlocked a door in a back hallway off the kitchen. A light flickered on as he did, illuminating a set of stairs that went down. Few homes in Nevada were built with basements, but he had purchased the ranch, in part, because it had a basement dug out of the stone underneath the property.

The land throughout the ranch was riddled with caves and tunnels. Some were natural, others had been dug as part of mine systems years earlier during the gold and silver rush. The mountains had been full of silver, though Ross had not heard of much gold in the area.

Once upon a time, the basement and the tunnels below the ranch were used to store alcohol during Prohibition. It only lasted for a few years in Nevada, but someone had made money off of it. After that, it was used to smuggle other goods, occasionally hold people captive, and sometimes as a discreet place to murder someone. Even Ross didn't know all the details. Many of the secrets had probably died with the previous owners.

Ross had been using the space as a storage facility for dangerous items. Sometime in the nineteen fifties, a previous owner built a series of vaults and shelters in the caverns. They were meant to withstand radioactive fallout. It just so happened that the vaults were also ideal for storing ghosts.

In his life, Bennett Ross had sold and shipped different things to make money. Guns were lucrative; so were drugs, but both came with a lot of baggage. There was a risk-versus-reward calculation that didn't always work out in his favor. On the other hand, ghosts were a unique item that fetched serious money and had no red tape attached.

It was not always easy to get ahold of a ghost. He had lost a few men over the years, especially during the early goings when he was getting used to what it meant. Finding people who could see ghosts and weren't afraid of them took time and effort as well.

The right spirit could fetch six figures. He heard of some selling back east for more than seven or eight. It depended on the buyer and what you had to sell. The ghost of a middle-aged baker who was hit by a car wasn't necessarily worth a lot, but the ghost of a Victorian-era serial killer that had a railroad spike driven through his head could be the exact thing some lunatic billionaire wanted to complete his collection at any cost.

The big score wasn't always what Ross was looking for. Other people dealt in that sort of thing. Various cults and paramilitary groups snatched up the violent and horrible ones quickly. But that middle-aged baker might be worth ten thousand to somebody. Collect a dozen of those, invest fifty bucks in lead-lined boxes, and the profits went through the roof.

Sales were just one of the benefits of the dead he had discovered in the Nevada deserts. Many had valuable secrets and information. A lot were more than willing to help somebody out in exchange for a favor or two. The dead, it seemed, were limited in how far they could travel and what effect they had on the real world. Some could be persuaded to do a lot for very little.

Ross crossed the basement when the overhead lights flickered. He stopped, waiting in the middle of the room as the hum of electricity became louder and then cut off entirely. He was left in the darkness, but he was not alone.

Something felt more than seen approached him in the shadows. The rush of cold air penetrated his clothes and made the hair on his arms stand on end. He didn't like it when they did that, but there was little he could do.

"We need to talk," Ross said.

Someone sighed in the dark. It was a soft sound, a drawn-out exhalation that sounded tired and maybe a little bored. Ross was used to the derision and sometimes the outright mockery. He ignored it and waited for a proper response.

"Why?"

The word was whispered right behind Ross' left ear. He flinched and tightened his shoulders. He didn't want to. He wouldn't have if he had any control, but he didn't. The reaction got the expected response. The soft voice laughed quietly.

"Glad you think this is funny," Ross said. "The FBI is looking around into those people you killed in the desert. If you're not careful, they're going to end your fun and games, and neither of us will have anything to show for it."

The cold air rushed over his shoulders, and he shuddered. He had not turned around because he knew there was nothing to see. If the ghost wanted to face him, it would have. Instead, they just played this game. It danced around him in the dark, it startled him, or froze him, or whatever other silly whim it wanted to fulfill at the moment. All he could do was explain the situation and hope it listened.

"Don't be a child," the ghost chided. "Send one of your boys, your little soldiers. Don't waste my time."

He felt the cold rushing around him. The ghost was going to leave him there, annoyed that he had shown up at all.

"It's not that easy." Ross interrupted the spirit's departure. "They already killed Patches."

He saw some movement then, nothing clear or distinct, but a definite sense that there was something in front of him. The cold rushed at his face this time, and he flinched again.

"Killed? What do you mean killed?"

The voice was right in his ear, with less mockery in its tone this time.

"He was watching the yard like always. They snuffed him. I don't know how, but he's gone. His item is torn up, too."

"How?" the voice demanded again.

"I told you I don't know. You're the expert here; you tell me. It looked like the bald guy grabbed him and just busted him. He's gone."

Something icy ran across the side of his face and down his neck below his collar. He raised his shoulders to force it away, but it didn't work. He spun away from the sensation, grasping at the freezing spot on his neck. Nothing was behind him, not that he expected to see anything in the dark. The sudden movement caused him to bang into a shelf and knock something to the floor.

"Jesus, I'm trying to help us out here," he protested.

"Who killed your little guard dog?" the voice in the dark asked.

"Someone working with this FBI agent. I don't know anything about him. I got a guy on them now. The agent's named Ventura. He's supposed to be here on vacation, but the locals pulled him into your mess. One phone call, and the Feds are here because you can't control your damn urges."

Another sound from the dark, soft but not a sigh this time. More of a hiss. Ross still had his hand on his neck, feeling the minor sting of the ghost's freezing touch on his throat. He didn't like working like this. He didn't like a ghost lording its power over him and treating him like a tool. His options were limited, though. At least for the foreseeable future.

"So?" the ghost said at last.

"What do you mean, 'So?'" Ross was unable to keep the anger from his tone. "Did you lose your brain when you died? This guy kills ghosts. You are a ghost. You want me to draw you a goddamn diagram of how that affects you?"

He took a step forward and then stopped abruptly, choking as a frozen hand closed around his neck and lifted him from the ground. There was still nothing to see and when he reached out, his hands felt nothing. It was like the darkness was choking him.

"Watch your tone, Bennett," the ghost whispered. "I will look for your bald man. Your FBI agent. But it's not free. You owe me."

The frozen hand released him, and he fell to the floor. Ross choked, grabbing his neck, and wincing at the feeling that seared through the outer layers of his flesh. He hoped the spirit hadn't left a mark. He didn't want to explain to others why he had a handprint around his throat.

"No, I got it," Ross said in a scratchy voice. "I know the deal."

"You best remember," the ghost assured him. "It stands until time runs out."

"I said I got it." Ross got to his feet. "These guys are going to come back. If my guy doesn't kill them, you need to. Nothing fancy. None of your silly games; just kill them quickly. You can do that, right?"

"I can show you," the voice said, in his ear once more and so close he felt the cold breath.

Ross flinched, and the voice in the dark laughed. The lights buzzed a moment later as they came back to life, and he was again alone in the basement. He cursed as he went back up the stairs. His business with the ghost couldn't come to an end soon enough. He was sick of him already and just wanted him to go away.

CHAPTER 13
SIN CITY

Ventura checked himself and Shane into a room at the MGM Grand. No one showed up at the casino after they'd made their way to the bar, so they ate dinner and had a couple of drinks while they waited to see if anything else happened. Nothing did.

The hotel had more than five thousand rooms. As much as Shane didn't like it, it was the perfect place to get lost. Nothing made for better camouflage than several thousand strangers.

Shane took a shower to get rid of some of the desert dust and a couple of days' worth of cross-country travel. When he got out, Ventura was on his laptop on one of the beds.

"I cannot find a damn thing on Bennett Ross," he explained, keeping his eyes on the screen.

"No criminal history?" Shane asked.

"Nothing that stuck. He was a person of interest in an ATF case that dealt with smuggled guns from Asia, but nothing came of it. That was thirty years ago."

"So, he's smarter than he looks. Good at covering his tracks," Shane said.

"Seems like it. I don't think he's ever been the brains of any operation, I think he's a way station. The ranch was raided for bootlegging back in the day, before the man was even born, but it might explain his interest in the place. This file says there are hidden caverns beneath the house."

"What year?"

"Nineteen twenty-five," Ventura answered.

It matched up with what Diamondfield had told Shane in the cemetery, but it was about as outdated as anything else he had heard. The ghosts were probably kept in the caverns, but that didn't help them much.

"In the fifties, they investigated the owner for mob ties. It was suspected of being a place where lower-level guys were taken to be murdered, but nothing came of that, either."

"And Ross isn't currently tied to organized crime?"

"Nothing. He's never been arrested for anything."

"So, in real terms, he's guilty of nothing, and we technically can't even be suspicious of him," Shane said.

"In a nutshell," Ventura agreed.

"But we know he's hoarding ghosts, and he probably tried to have me killed. And there's just as good a chance he knows I can destroy ghosts now."

"We need to catch him off-guard somewhere," Ventura said. "Find out what we can about this killer ghost."

"So, follow Bennett next time he leaves?"

"We need to dig up some more on him. There has to be a reason for all those ghosts. He could be selling them, using them to fight, or to plan heists—something. He has to be conducting business somewhere and with someone."

"And if the second shooter is with him?" Shane asked.

"They won't see us coming this time. This isn't my first stakeout."

Shane sat on his bed and stared out the window. They had a view of the Strip, and the lights made it look as bright as midday outside even though it was the middle of the night.

"What's the plan?" He looked at the agent.

If they were going to run it like a proper investigation, Ventura had more experience in that regard. He was willing to let the other man take the lead, at least for the more mundane and technical aspects.

"Wait 'til morning," Ventura said. "We'll be less suspicious driving around during the day, and it'll give me time to find a new car. I don't think Ross is going anywhere this time of night, anyway. He knows his assassin failed, that we've been to his house, and that you destroyed one of his ghosts. He's going to be on edge, so we need to give him some time to relax and formulate his plan. Then when he thinks he's on top of things and leaves the ranch, we'll be there to tail him."

"This all a plan to get more of your overpriced toast in the morning?" Shane closed the curtain and laid back on his pillow.

"Jesus, it was a buffet. There was more than toast," Ventura said.

"Whatever you say," Shane replied.

He closed his eyes and drifted off while Ventura worked on his computer, making the arrangements he thought they would need for the next morning and their attack on Bennett Ross.

The sun was barely up when Shane woke and prepared to leave. Ventura was asleep in the next bed, his computer still open and several handwritten notes piled around it on the sheets.

Shane didn't know how late the other man had worked, but it didn't matter. If they planned to catch Ross as he went about his business, they needed to head out early and make sure they could catch him.

"Hey, time to go." Shane tossed a pillow at the agent.

Ventura sat up, reaching for his gun with one hand while Shane laughed and backed away.

"Hate to see the condition of your alarm clock," he said.

"Sorry." Ventura let go of the weapon. "What time is it?"

"It's Vegas. Does it matter?"

"Guess not," the agent conceded. "I got us a new car. If anyone followed us in, they won't catch us on the way out."

Ventura took a moment to freshen up before they headed out. He even ignored the breakfast buffet on their way to pick up their new car, which he had dropped off at the hotel.

Since he had rented the vehicle, Ventura insisted on driving, and they were back on the road before the sun rose over the casinos. The city seemed as busy as ever. Maybe the traffic was a little diminished, but plenty of people were still out and about. The time of day didn't matter; someone was always doing something in Las Vegas.

Many of the ghosts Shane had seen the night before were gone, but a few were still there. The ones on the streets he had seen on their way in had barely moved overnight. Whatever had happened to them, and whatever kept them bound to the streets of Las Vegas, they weren't keen on fighting it or looking for greener pastures. They were permanent fixtures, just like the lights, fountains, signs, and marquees.

"What happens in Vegas really does stay here," Shane said, watching a spirit outside of the Cosmopolitan.

"What do you mean?" Ventura asked.

"The dead. They just hang out on the streets."

"That's weird, right?" Ventura asked. "Most go and haunt places or something, don't they?"

Shane found it amusing how little Ventura seemed to know about ghosts even though he could see them and was interested in investigating them. He had spent too much of his life denying they were real, and in doing so had failed to observe them very well. He had learned everything he didn't want to know about them and nothing that he did.

"Some haunt. Some hide. Some wander. I guess these guys loiter. It is weird, though, to be out in public and just standing around. Maybe they like the crowds."

"Most don't though, right? They want to keep away from the living?"

"I don't know about most. Some. You know Herbert's a personable guy. He likes crowds. He was more mobile in the circus, though. Liked to travel, see new people and places."

"Yeah," Ventura agreed.

"One thing to remember about ghosts—and maybe it's hard after dealing with ones like Mr. Shadow and whatever that thing was that haunted you as a kid—is that they are just people. You know a guy who likes chicken wings and football? His ghost is basically going to be the same guy."

"Basically?" Ventura said.

Shane shrugged. They passed another spirit outside of the Venetian just standing in front of the doors like he was waiting to get in.

"Death can fracture a person a little bit. Or a lot. Herbert is very normal for a ghost. I bet he was the same guy when he was alive. Eloise has a sharpness to her. I don't know what kind of little girl she was, but I bet she never killed anyone. She can do that now. Something broke in her when she died. Same thing with the Davis Sisters. Even Carl."

"Do you trust them?" Ventura asked.

"Of course," Shane replied. "But should *you*? Not fully. Not yet."

The agent laughed like he thought Shane was joking, but stopped when he realized he was serious.

"You're telling me if I go to your house, there's a chance one of your ghosts would kill me? Even though they know I'm your friend?"

"I don't think it'd happen. It wouldn't be Carl unless you did something to provoke him. They're the people they used to be, only more in some ways and less in others. You could think of it like when a dog goes feral. There's something untamed and unpredictable in there, and you need to always keep that in mind, although it's smooth sailing most of the time. If a ghost doesn't immediately try to kill you, there's a good chance it never will."

"Do you have a percentage there? We're in Vegas. Maybe some odds?"

"Trust your gut, Ventura. You deal with criminals, it's sort of the same. Not everyone wants to shoot you, right?"

"Hope not," he said.

"Point is, if you want to do this kind of work, you need to look at them like people. Treat them like people. If they push you, then sure, you might have to destroy them. But it doesn't always come to that."

"Easy for you to say," Ventura pointed out. "You can destroy them. I can't do anything."

"You can fight. You know how to use iron, and you know how far you need to go to get away. You know about lead and salt. That's more than a lot of people get."

"Still makes me nervous as hell. The really dangerous ones, I don't think I can survive something like that. Mr. Shadow would have turned me into one of those Hounds. This desert killer…"

"Everyone survives until they don't," Shane said.

"Not a comfort. At all," Ventura told him.

Shane lit a cigarette and nodded. Ventura was silent for a long moment, and Shane caught him looking furtively in his direction every so often.

"Something else on your mind?" he asked finally.

"I've heard some things. Over the years, I mean. I know some ghosts can be friendly or helpful. Like Herbert. Or the ones at your house."

He glanced at Shane and let the statement hang, and Shane waited for him to get to the point.

"You said you trust them. But how much? Do you ever get a feeling they're holding something back?"

Shane exhaled out the window, letting the hot desert air pull the smoke from the car.

"Everyone holds something back, don't they? Living or dead. Not sure that's a thing to worry about."

"Right," Ventura said.

As an FBI agent, he'd mastered an indifference in conversing with others, a way to hide his intentions, but Shane was certain he was angling toward something.

"Ask what you want to ask," Shane said after another brief pause.

"What do you mean?"

Ventura's eyes were on the road. He was looking disinterested now, and Shane was suspicious.

"We're working together here, Ventura. Don't play games."

He didn't like someone being coy about their intentions, and Ventura had never struck him as that kind of man. Something was eating at the younger man.

"What do you know about possession?" Ventura asked bluntly.

Shane took another long drag of his cigarette, watching the other man now. His eyes were straight forward.

"I think I should be asking you that question," Shane replied.

Ventura said nothing and breathed in more sharply than necessary.

"This was long before I saw Herbert come out of the woman in Burkitt. Back then I thought it was a demon like in movies. But I saw it, it went into someone and took them over. Wore them like a suit and made them do what they wanted. Part of me knew it was a ghost. But I didn't know it could be done, so I assumed it was a demon. Until I saw Herbert do it too."

"Yeah?" Shane asked. "When was that?"

"Long time ago. When I was a kid."

"Who got possessed?"

Ventura rolled his shoulders awkwardly.

"A family friend. He was old and sick. People thought he was just crazy, you know? He had some early-onset dementia and was not himself by then. But I saw a ghost just… go into him. Use him."

"It happens," Shane explained. "Not often. It's not easy for them. A healthy, living person is like a hurricane to a ghost, pushing back hard. They need to fight their way in. A sick person makes it easier. Or a drunk. Lower defenses and not enough energy to keep up that fight."

"But what if someone let them in?" he asked.

Shane raised an eyebrow.

"You mean, just a regular person letting their guard down and allowing a ghost in?"

"Yeah. Does that ever happen?"

"It does. I once let a ghost possess me to experience having a smoke again." Shane grinned.

Ventura looked at him to check if he was serious.

"What the—?"

They both laughed before Shane continued, "But if your friend had dementia, I doubt it worked the same way."

"Yeah," Ventura said. "Just thought it was weird when I saw it."

Shane grunted, and Ventura slowed the car. They were coming up to a rest stop and gas station off the main road that led to the ranch. If Ross went to the city, they'd see him pass in his conspicuous car.

CHAPTER 14
THE BUSINESS OF DEATH

Just before nine in the morning, the cherry red Cadillac Eldorado with personalized plates drove past the rest stop on its way to Las Vegas. Ventura was on the road moments after, two cars separating them from Ross.

Ross was alone. Shane didn't think he had been the second gunman, so a third man was still out there somewhere, and they needed to be on the lookout. He checked the mirror multiple times as they drove and saw no sign they were being followed.

Ventura was adept at tailing the other car at a distance, keeping at least two vehicles between them as they headed into Las Vegas. Ross headed not to the Strip but to the Rampart Casino off the beaten path near a golf resort.

A valet took Ross' Cadillac, and the man got out and headed into the casino in no hurry. Ventura and Shane followed shortly after, keeping out of sight as they watched Ross head to the Market Place Buffet, where he sat at a table with three other men who had been waiting some time for him, judging by the meals they were already eating.

Ventura watched from a distance and snapped a few casual photos on his phone while Ross settled in, talking to the other men.

"I know that guy," Shane said.

One man had his back to him, but of the other two, one was instantly familiar.

"Which guy?" Ventura asked.

"Skinny one on the left in the dumb polo shirt. He's from Boston.

Member of the Endless Night."

The four men talked, with Ross doing most of the work while the others listened. Shane didn't know the man's name, but he recognized him from Randall West's home. West was the head of the Cult of the Endless Night throughout New England until his death. Shane was an unwilling guest in his home for a time, trapped in a cage designed to hold ghosts. West had invited guests, and the man sitting with Ross was one of them.

Most of West's guests had died that night when one of the ghosts from West's collection had run amok. The Endless Night had been all but destroyed, but there were still stragglers.

"One on the right is another made guy from Philly. He used to work with your dead hitman, Canterino. His name's Luke Parisi. I thought he was still in prison, but here we are."

"So, we've got mob guys and cultists. What's the glue holding it together?" Shane asked.

He understood the Endless Night, but the mob was a curveball. He just couldn't imagine any traditional organized crime outfit suddenly getting into the dead. Everything he knew about the mob made him think they'd want nothing to do with ghosts if they could avoid it.

"I guess it's the ghosts. It has to be, right?"

"What does the Philadelphia mob want ghosts from Nevada for?" Shane asked.

Ventura did not have an answer that made sense. They'd seen the dead mobster at the ranch, so maybe that was a link. Someone wanted to check in with old friends. It was a nonsensical thought at best, though.

The man with his back to Ventura and Shane was talking as the others listened. Ross told him something and he pulled out his phone.

"Looks like a banking app." Ventura watched closely and took more photos.

The man pressed a few buttons, and Ventura grunted.

"Big transfer," Ventura said, zooming in with his phone. Fifty thousand dollars was being sent to someone for something.

"Business buffet," Shane said. "Probably bought a ghost or two."

"Maybe," Ventura said. "Can't arrest someone for that, unfortunately."

Ross checked his phone, and then after a few more minutes, the two men shook hands. Ross said goodbye to the other two and the group split up, with only the cultist remaining at the table to finish eating his meal.

"Let's stay on Ross," Ventura said, though Shane had no intention of going after the others.

They followed Ross at a distance across the casino floor, staying out of sight. The man who had made the transfer did not leave with him. Either Ross was going back to the ranch, or something else was being put together. Shane wanted to see what he had sold and maybe find out what the other man planned to do with it.

Shane and Ventura held back as Ross waited at the front of the casino for the valet to retrieve his car. They watched from behind a vacant slot machine, the sounds of the casino loud and obnoxious even at that early hour.

Ventura moved toward the doors as the red car pulled up and Ross walked to the driver's side door, but he was waylaid by a man in a dark jacket blocking the path.

"Need you to dial it back a touch, lads," the man said with a faint British accent.

He wore gloves, and one gloved hand barely concealed the gun he held in the other, pointed at Ventura's gut.

Shane stopped and locked eyes with the man, who smiled at him.

"I know what you're thinking. Maybe you could make a move before I turn the gun on you, yeah? But I won't, you see. I'll kill your friend where he stands and then take my chances with you. You already know I'm a good shot. You saw what I did to Nicky in the parking lot."

"I did," Shane said. The shot had been as accurate as anyone could have made it, right through the skull from far enough away that Shane had not even seen the man take it.

"You're going to kill us on the casino floor?" Ventura asked.

"If you make me," the man replied. "I think that's your choice. Or we could go over there to the men's room and have a chat like gentlemen. What do you say?"

He nodded toward the nearest restroom, and Ventura turned without saying anything. Shane joined him, and the trio walked across the casino without drawing any suspicion. Ventura entered the room first, and Shane followed. The British hitman came up behind them and closed the door after him.

He kept the gun trained on Shane and Ventura and walked to the far side of the restroom and back, looking into stalls to see if anyone was there. They waited in silence for a couple of men to finish, wash their hands, and leave.

When the room was clear, the man pointed his gun at Ventura's head.

"Let's see some hands," he said.

Ventura and Shane obliged, raising their hands while the man took something from his pocket to wedge the door shut so they would not be disturbed.

"You're FBI, but you're not working out here; I know that." He turned the gun on Shane. "But who the hell are you?"

"Not much of a gambler, but I love the shows," Shane replied.

"Comedy will get your brains splattered on that mirror," the gunman said.

"We're here investigating a series of murders in the desert," Ventura interrupted. "There are still three missing people out there."

"But you're not investigating are you, Agent Ventura? We looked into you, and there is no FBI involvement in those cases. You're not even supposed to be on assignment right now. You're on vacation," the Brit said.

"Guess I don't need to tell you anything anymore," Ventura said.

Shane had no idea how Ross and his thug could have learned so much about Ventura's involvement outside of having a contact in the FBI. That put Ventura and Shane in a very vulnerable position.

"We got you on camera breaking onto the ranch property," the man said.

He returned his attention to Shane.

"And we caught you engaging in some very interesting behavior. So why not tell me who you're working for and what you're doing here?"

Shane shrugged.

"Came from Boston," he said. "We're consolidating and rebuilding now that West is dead. The Endless Night needs to get its former strength back and fast. We need to be sure of who we're working with. Can't risk getting involved with the wrong people again."

The gunman grinned and cocked the hammer on the weapon.

"I thought all you Americans loved my accent because it makes me sound smart, but here you are talking to me like I'm an idiot," he said. "You're not Endless Night, lad. Not by a long shot. They already had their showcase. You're something else."

The bathroom door rattled before Shane could reply. Whatever the man had used to seal it failed and clattered to the floor as the door pushed open. The distraction was brief, but it was enough.

Ventura moved without hesitation. He was closer to the gunman, and his reaction time was impressive even to Shane. He forced the gun up and away and tried to disarm the Brit in one swift motion, but the assassin's grip was solid. They struggled over the gun, and Ross' man jerked them both roughly to the side, using Ventura's body to hit Shane before he could join the fight.

The hitman raised a booted foot and planted his heel brutally into Ventura's gut, knocking him back into Shane and causing them both to stumble. Ventura kept the gun tight in his grip, and the Brit was forced to let it go as the sudden jerk was more than he could withstand.

The gun clattered across the floor as Shane caught Ventura, stopping him from falling but moving back several paces so they could maintain their balance.

The man who had just entered the restroom, an elderly gambler in khaki shorts with a fanny pack, was caught by surprise. He froze when the gunman grabbed him, producing a short-bladed knife from inside his jacket and pressing the mirrored blade tightly against the stranger's throat. The Brit wrapped his free arm around the man's chest and took a step backward toward the door.

"There we go, lads. You just stay here and take a moment to yourselves, lest you want to be cleaning this poor fella's blood off your shoes."

The hostage mumbled something, tears welling in his eyes as his captor pulled him another step closer to the exit.

Ventura's gun was already in his hands, pointed down but ready.

"You're not leaving here with that man," he said.

The Brit grinned.

"I bet he'd rather leave here with me and stay alive than have me slit his throat when you try to save him. What do you reckon, Granddad?"

The man whimpered, and the Brit squeezed him tighter.

"That's settled, then. Keep your distance." He pushed the bathroom door open with his foot and slipped out.

"He's not getting out of here," Ventura said to Shane. "Need you to hang back while I handle this."

Shane let Ventura take the lead, lifting his hands in mock surrender.

"By all means, Agent Ventura. Go lay down the law."

Ventura nodded and followed the Brit and his hostage out the door. Shane was only a step behind.

CHAPTER 15

DEAD MAN WALKING

Someone was already screaming before Ventura was on the casino floor. A woman at a slot machine near the restrooms had seen the knife at the elderly man's throat as the British man dragged him toward the door.

It took a moment for the panic to spread. A scream in a casino was not always an unexpected sound, but the other patrons soon keyed in that it was not the delighted screams of a winner. People bolted, running for what they considered relative safety as the hitman dragged his hostage toward the exit.

"You need to stop. Now." Ventura aimed his weapon at the man.

He knew he could make the shot if the man didn't move, but he also knew he wouldn't risk it. If something went wrong, the hostage would die. He was bluffing, at least for now, but he hoped the hitman didn't want to call him on it.

"Now, now, Agent Ventura, I thought I was clear. You stay there, I leave, and this fella survives. If that's not the game we're playing, just say so, and I'll bleed him right here on this ugly carpet."

"It'll be your blood, too, the moment you do," Ventura said.

"Then that's what we call a stalemate, innit?"

"Drop the knife," a man behind the Brit yelled, coming in through the front doors of the casino with a gun drawn. He looked like casino security to Ventura, and a second man soon joined him, his gun trained not on the Brit but on Ventura.

"On the floor, now," the second man yelled.

"My name is Xander Ventura. I'm with the FBI," Ventura shouted.

"This man has taken a hostage, so how about we focus on him instead."

The security guard looked at his partner but kept his gun on Ventura.

"Drop the gun, and we'll sort out who's who," the guard said.

"As soon as he drops the knife and releases the hostage. He's already killed one man this week outside of the Golden Gate Towers hotel."

He kept one hand on the gun, keeping the hitman in his sights, and reached into his pocket with the other, digging out his ID. He tossed it at the closest security guard.

"Read it," he said.

The guard bent down and picked up his badge and ID, looking it over carefully and then showing it to the other security guard.

"Looks real," he said.

"Of course it's real. You think I made a fake government ID to hold this guy at a standoff in a golf casino?"

"If anyone cares, I'm planning to leave in the next two minutes, or this man's death is on your hands. Either we both die, or you let us both go, choice is yours," the hitman said.

"Please," the hostage muttered, a thin line of blood already visible on his throat where the blade had dug into him.

Ventura waved for the security officers to back off. He didn't know how much he trusted the assassin's word, but he had no doubt that he would kill the old man if pressed. Whether he was willing to die alongside him didn't matter.

The security guards were reluctant to back off. The hitman dragged his hostage toward the exit, turning enough so that he could see the guard behind him and the gun he had drawn.

"Security man, you sure you want to risk it? You think you're going to keep your job here after you get a valuable customer killed? What's your name, Granddad?"

He gave the hostage a shake and pressed onto his throat again.

"Earl," the old man said, his voice hoarse. "Earl Mooney."

"Earl Mooney," the hitman repeated boisterously. "Anyone in here know Earl Mooney? Wife? Best friend? Anyone?"

"My wife… she's in the room still. She's sleeping," Earl said.

"Aww, that's a shame. You won't get to say goodbye before I cut your goddamn throat because this asshole security guard didn't want to get out of my way."

"Let him go," Ventura shouted at the guard. The man complied, a half-panicked look in his eyes. He lowered his weapon and backed away from the door.

The Brit smiled at Ventura, holding Earl tighter than ever.

"Look at that, an assist from the FBI. Much appreciated, Agent Ventura. Maybe you're not a bad one after all, eh?"

The hitman pulled his hostage toward the automatic doors, which slid open behind him, leading to the front driveway and valet parking. He kept his back to the outside, eyes moving from the security guards to Ventura and back.

"What's going to happen here is we're going to get in a car. Mr. Mooney is going to be my driver, and I will sit in the back with this knife on his throat as I tell him where to go. You'll wait here until we're out of sight. Don't doubt that I can bleed him and take the wheel before you can catch up with me, so be smart lads, yeah?"

Ventura paced the man slowly and steadily, watching him back up toward the driveway in front of the casino. He said nothing as Shane Ryan approached from the hitman's right, the long, white porcelain lid from a toilet tank grasped firmly in his hands.

Shane must have slipped out a different door after they left the bathroom. Ventura had not even noticed he was no longer behind him, and the hitman had not given him another thought in his efforts to escape.

The Brit kept talking, explaining what was going to happen and how he'd let Earl Mooney survive if they listened to him and did what he instructed. Shane moved stealthily. He didn't wait for a signal from anyone, didn't acknowledge the security guards or Ventura with their guns drawn. He hefted the porcelain lid and brought it down squarely on the hitman's head.

The porcelain shattered with a loud crunch, breaking into several large pieces. The hitman's body spasmed, and the knife fell. Mr. Mooney collapsed, holding his throat and choking.

Shane dropped to the ground as the assassin fell in a heap, blood running down his face from a wound in his head. He was unconscious before he hit the pavement, but Shane planted a knee in the small of his back anyway, pushing the knife away and restraining the man's arms.

A flurry of movement followed as Ventura joined Shane, cuffing the hitman while others attended to Mr. Mooney. Police sirens grew louder, and Shane backed off without protest as Ventura checked the hitman's neck for a pulse.

"He's not dead, is he?" Shane asked.

Dozens of gamblers were taking photos. Shane had angled away from them, his back to the casino, and Ventura shook his head. The man had a steady pulse, but the toilet tank lid had busted his skull open badly. He was bleeding profusely and would need medical attention.

Mr. Mooney was fine other than the stress of the event and a thin slice in his neck. One of the security guards returned Ventura's ID and informed him that an ambulance and police had been called, though the sirens made that much obvious.

"That could have gone south," Ventura pointed out as he joined Shane a few paces from the downed and cuffed man.

"As in he could have died, or it wouldn't have worked? Because I've been hit with one of those before, and it was always going to work," Shane said.

"I stand corrected," Ventura said.

It took longer than he wanted to go over the incident with the police. Two of the detectives who responded had also responded to the murder at Shane's hotel and recognized Shane and Ventura from that incident. Explaining the presence of the second man and almost another corpse was met with a degree of skepticism from Las Vegas law enforcement.

While the assassin had not succeeded in killing anyone or getting information out of Shane or Ventura, he had slowed them once more. Ross was long gone, either back home or on to do more business with other contacts in town, and it was unlikely they would catch up with him again to see what he was up to.

The police took them back to the station to give statements, along with the security guards and Mr. Mooney after he received medical attention. At least two dozen people on the scene attested to the bravery of both Ventura and Shane, which, along with corroborating security footage, gave them a little leeway in dealing with the cops.

It was early the next morning by the time they were free to go. Ventura was frustrated that they were knocked back every time they made progress. Ross could have cleaned his whole inventory out by then, sold whatever he was selling, and left the state if he had wanted to.

"Normally, caving some jackass' skull in is a high point of my day, but this has been a bust," Shane said when the two were reunited in the hall outside of the interrogation rooms.

He had pulled a cigarette from one of his seemingly endless supply of packs and already had it in his mouth when one of the detectives stopped them.

"Agent Ventura," the woman said. Her name was Gleeson, and she had been the first to soften to the idea of him and Shane when she found out what they had done. "Got some information on your hitman."

Shane stopped to listen as she held up a folder.

"Name is Dennis Barclay. Former British Army, Special Reconnaissance Regiment. Left the service about ten years ago. Been in the U.S. for most of that time but off the radar. Not even a traffic ticket since he had his passport stamped. Gun he had was unregistered."

"No ties to the victim from the hotel parking lot?" Ventura asked.

"Nothing," the detective replied. "Just thought you'd like to know."

"Yeah, thanks, Detective," he said as she left them.

Even if the mob connection didn't make sense to him yet, it was a connection. Ross had met with someone from Philly and had sent Canterino after Shane at his hotel. How did a former British soldier fit into that?

"You look lost," Shane said.

"I am. Why was this guy here? Special Reconnaissance Regiment? That's covert spying, special forces stuff. And he's working for a Nevada ghost farmer?"

"Ex-military," Shane pointed out. "He could just be a contract killer these days. Could be a Reaper. Could be Endless Night. They hire mercenaries, and he seemed to know about them."

"That's the problem. Everything we run into could be three other things. We're not getting any answers, and no matter who he's working for, none of this gets us back to why we came here. We've got a killer in the desert who's not alive," Ventura said.

Shane started toward the exit, pulling out his Zippo lighter as he walked. He led them outside before stopping at the doors to light the cigarette and take a dramatic inhale before speaking.

"We need to go back to the desert," he said. "Not the ranch, the desert. Your map show anyone else in our radius? Houses, ranches, anyone besides Ross and his outfit?"

"A few, yeah." Ventura pulled out his phone and looked over the pins he'd placed on his map. "It's mostly dead out there, but there are a few houses that seem abandoned and some trailers. Maybe a half-dozen total. Never saw anything at any of them before."

"How hard did you look?" Shane asked.

"Probably not hard enough," Ventura conceded.

He had not seen any ghosts at the properties, just empty space, but that didn't mean no ghosts were there. He wasn't sure what Shane was getting at, but he would try anything if it helped them get ahead of this case instead of constantly tripping up.

CHAPTER 16

BONE DRY

The sun was low in the west by the time they arrived at the stretch of desert where the murders had taken place, on the far side of the canyon, away from Ross' ranch. From the road, there was little to see for a great distance before Ventura took a left down a forgotten dirt road toward a ramshackle house with an ancient-looking farm windmill on a rusted steel frame out front.

The house was all but stripped of whatever paint had once covered it, worn away by years of sand blasting the panels, and the windows had long ago been broken out.

"I feel like an idiot doing this," Ventura said as they pulled up in front of the house.

"Investigating an abandoned house?" Shane finished a cigarette and pinched it out before fieldstripping.

"No. Dropping Ross like this. It's driving me crazy. The man is guilty of something. Probably a lot of things. But my hands are tied. Ghost trafficking? Not a crime. I can't report anything I've seen so far because the evidence was illegally obtained, and it's also stuff that would get me committed to a psych facility if I brought it up. It's frustrating. It's goddamn... frustrating."

He slammed a hand on the steering wheel to accent the point.

"It can be," Shane agreed.

"You're as calm as a cat by the fire. How does this not get to you? I get that you're better at this than me, and you've been doing it longer, but how do you not just lose your goddamn mind when you get arrested for something you didn't do? When you can never tell anyone the truth because it makes you seem even guiltier?"

Shane smiled and shook his head.

"You're still thinking like a cop, Agent Ventura. If you keep doing that, you will never survive."

"What does that mean? I *am* a cop, Ryan. I'm a field agent with the FBI. I catch criminals for a living. I solve crimes and hunt bad guys. I do what you do, but for the living, and I just don't know how to switch to this insane nightmare of a world."

"You don't switch because there's nothing to switch to. It's the same world. That's what you need to wrap your head around. No one at that casino today lives in a world where a British special forces soldier almost slices Earl Mooney's head off outside a breakfast buffet. But they did today, just for a minute. They stepped into your world, and you were on top of it because it's what you're used to. And maybe I'm more used to the dead than you, but you can still walk among the graves without me. It's all the same," Shane said.

"Then why do we keep dropping the ball on this? You've almost been killed twice, and we're no closer to solving these murders or shutting Ross down."

Shane snorted and opened the car door, getting out and squinting as a wind picked up, blasting fine grains of sand into his face.

"I was not almost killed twice. People threatened to kill me twice. There's a difference," he explained.

"I'm not joking, Ryan." Ventura joined him outside the abandoned house.

"Neither am I. This isn't supposed to be easy. It'd be great if it was. You show up, your murderous ghost is right there, you pop his head like a jack-o'-lantern on November first, and you go home. Great. They don't usually let you do that, though. You have to hunt. You have to get dirty. And sometimes, you almost die. Sometimes, people *do* die."

"But you have to do it alone. There's no backup. No one to tell the story to when you're done. You're like a ghost yourself," Ventura said.

Shane started toward the house.

"I'm not alone. I let you tag along."

He understood what Ventura was getting at but had little wisdom to share. He needed to figure out how to deal with the problems that arose from navigating a world full of ghosts. If he couldn't reconcile the fact that he would be flying blind a lot and in precarious or dangerous situations with no one else to rely on, things were not going to work.

Shane had always heard that the best way to learn something was immersion. He approached the door to the house and pulled, taking it clean off the hinges as the dry, rotten wood gave way with little resistance.

The inside of the house was sparse. Much of what had once been there had been removed, though there were still some chairs and a wobbly-looking card table. Old bottles and cans were tossed around haphazardly along with stacks of old papers and magazines. There were signs of people having lived there, probably squatters, but nothing looked recent. Dust covered it all, and the fine grit of the desert sand was in every room and hallway they checked.

No spirits wandered the halls, and the house had no basement. The two men left it behind and followed Ventura's map to the next house, tucked away in some Mesquite thickets down in a shallow valley not far from the first house.

The second house was in better condition than the first but not by much. The windows had not been smashed out so there was less dust inside, although there was still an impressive amount.

Shane wondered if any of the desert land still had value. The abandoned houses had to be from a time when there was still hope of finding gold or silver in the mountains. He wondered how many years they had been empty.

Whatever had happened to the owners, it did not seem like they had died there. No ghosts haunted the second house that they checked, or the third. Neither the killer ghost nor any hapless, forgotten desert spirit waited for them. There was only sand and shadows.

"That's it for the houses, but there are some trailers," Ventura said when they returned to the car.

Night was nearly upon them. Shane wondered if their killer ghost was out there watching them futilely go from empty house to empty house, amusing itself with their wasted efforts. Some ghosts were jerks like that.

Ventura had to leave the roads and drive across the barren desert to their next destination, an old seventies-era Beeline trailer parked in the middle of nowhere on flat, rotted tires. Years of sun exposure and blowing sand had bleached whatever the original paint color was to a faded, creamy yellow.

A picnic table was set up outside the trailer alongside old piles of junk like scrap metal, the bench seat from the rear of a van, and several old oil drums. A tattered canvas awning was held up by one crooked pole and half torn away from the roof of the trailer on the other end.

A face appeared out of the trailer window, watching them as they approached. It was deadly thin and pale, not the face of someone living. The sunken eyes were almost invisible in the dark pools of the ghost's skull.

Ventura parked a short distance away, putting a greater distance between the car and the trailer than he had with the houses they had visited. He could see the ghost as clearly as Shane could, and his sense of caution had taken over.

Shane got out of the car and looked around the trailer before proceeding. It was nearly collapsed into the sand, thanks to the flat tires, but there was still room beneath it for something to hide. Nothing seemed to be hidden in the shadows, however, and the ghost in the trailer made no move to hide itself, either. It watched them from the window, its eyes full of anxiety.

"You coming out?" Shane shouted to the ghost.

He didn't want to go into the trailer, given the state of it. The idea of falling through a rotten floor or getting tetanus didn't appeal to him.

The ghost's eyes widened, making them more visible and oddly more horrifying. They looked yellow and rheumy like they were coated with a layer of syrup.

Shane lit another cigarette and the ghost slowly drifted out from the walls of the trailer, staying in the shadows of the half awning. Now that he was fully in view, it looked like he might have died in the trailer after a long bout of some sickness. His age was impossible to gauge given his state, all jaundiced skin and bones, pocked with sores and scrapes.

"Who are you?" The ghost's voice was reminiscent of the howling desert wind that rushed under the trailer now and then and created a haunting whisper.

"Name's Shane Ryan," he answered, lighting a cigarette. "You been here long?"

"Long," the ghost agreed with a nod.

His neck and shoulders were so thin that he looked like a bobblehead.

"I'm Dale. My name. Dale," the ghost said.

He stayed half hidden behind the awning, darkness keeping most of his frail frame from view.

"All right, Dale. Have you heard that some people have died around here recently? People lost out in the desert?"

"I died out here," Dale replied.

He pointed a long, bony finger at the trailer but kept his eyes on Shane.

"Died in there. Long time now."

"I'm getting that," Shane said. "More recent though. Last few weeks. A ghost has been killing them. You see any ghosts around here who might do something like that?"

Although they had not spoken for very long, Shane had been

119

suspicious of Dale at first. Now that he could see and interact with him, he didn't think they had found their murderer. Dale looked creepy, but it was hard not to if you died alone in a trailer in the desert, Shane thought. The way he interacted with them, the way he spoke and cowered behind the awning, didn't say cold-blooded killer to Shane at all.

"Jack," Dale said, violently nodding again. He turned and looked out at the darkening desert. "His name's Jack."

"The ghost? The one that's been killing people?" Ventura asked, finally coming closer.

Dale looked at him for the first time, wide-eyed and surprised as though he hadn't noticed him.

"He'll be out soon. Doesn't like the light," the ghost said.

"Where can we find Jack?" Shane asked.

Dale pointed his bony finger out at nothing.

"Out there. He hates thieves. He'll find you if you steal from him. You can't have his treasure."

"Can you be a little more specific for us?" Shane asked.

The sun had set beyond the ridge, and the desert was swiftly being swallowed in shadows. Stars were already visible in the sky, but Dale stayed hidden behind his awning as though it protected him.

"He wanders," Dale said. "He has to keep his treasure safe. He told me to never look for it."

"When did he tell you that?" Shane asked.

Dale shook his head and receded into the shadows. Only the faint glimmer of his sunken eyes remained, deep in the shadow below the awning.

"He'll leave you in the sand where the desert can eat you. Scour you clean down to your bones, dry and dusty. You don't want that. You don't want to die in the dust. It hurts to breathe when you die in the dust."

The two eyes faded from view. Shane took a step forward, his cigarette extinguished once more and hanging from his lips as the dry wind pulled at it and whipped around them. The awning caught in the breeze and flapped, exposing the empty space where Dale had just been. The ghost was gone.

"Jack has a treasure. That mean anything to you?" Shane asked.

"Not really," Ventura said, using a small flashlight to scan the area around the trailer. "Are we just letting him go?"

"He doesn't want to talk anymore. I wouldn't provoke him."

"You think he's telling the truth about this Jack?"

"Think so," Shane said. "What can you do with a first name and a one-mile radius?"

"We're about to find out," he answered.

The wind spattered the trailer with sand, the sound like an irregular static in Shane's ears. The light over the horizon was gone as they got back into the car. He saw Dale's face in the window again, only for a moment, peering from the shadows beneath the trailer. His eyes met Shane's one last time before the darkness swallowed him.

CHAPTER 17
BLOOD MONEY

Ventura was back at his laptop, intermittently hitting keys and then scrolling and hitting keys again. Shane let him do his work while smoking and watching more stars appear in the sky.

He caught sight of the moon, the thinnest crescent, partially obscured behind a scant covering of clouds just as Ventura turned the monitor toward him.

"Jack Dallas." Shane read from the file that Ventura had pulled up from an FBI database.

"Casino boss during the mob era. Allegedly stole the entire take from the count room one night, supposedly several million. Had the mob and the FBI looking for him, but he was never seen again after the heist, and the money was never recovered. That's Jack, and that's a treasure," Ventura said.

"How do we know he didn't just leave with the money and retire to a tropical island?" Shane countered.

"We don't," Ventura conceded. "But he's the only Jack I've got with a treasure. The FBI never found him, but if the mob did, they wouldn't publicize it. Suppose they caught him and buried him out here but never found the cash."

"And now, his ghost kills anyone he thinks is getting close to it. Still doesn't explain why this is happening now if they did him in more than half a century ago."

If Jack Dallas was their ghost, his death must have done something to keep him hidden. Or maybe someone had disturbed him recently, and that had set him off on a paranoid path to kill what he thought were treasure hunters after his loot. They'd have to find the ghost to know for sure.

"Another mob ghost points us back toward Ross," Shane said. "Maybe he died elsewhere, and Ross brought him back here to cage him, and then let him go for some reason."

"Maybe," Ventura agreed. "Or he escaped. I still don't understand the cage thing."

He read more of the document on his laptop before shutting it down and returning it to the back seat.

"Dallas used to run the Emerald Casino. That's where he pulled the heist. The Emerald was torn down in the early two thousands, but it's the same location where Avignon Casino is today."

Shane nodded, exhaling smoke out the window.

"Maybe someone there knows something about Dallas. All the casinos I've seen so far have a ghost or two loitering around."

Ventura turned on the car and looked back at the trailer.

"You want to check out the other couple of trailers or head back to the Avignon?"

"Let's do Avignon," Shane said. "I don't think Jack is hiding in a trailer. I think he's out there like Dale said, wandering the desert and protecting his heist money."

Ventura turned the car around, heading back toward the main road. He checked the mirrors regularly, as though the ghost might appear in one running after them.

"A few million bucks in long-forgotten stolen cash could be good motivation for Ross to let a ghost run free," Shane suggested as they drove. "Maybe he's tracking the ghost, same as us. Or he found the money, and that's why people are dying now. Stole his treasure, and Jack got pissed."

"Wouldn't he just kill Ross?" Ventura asked.

"Only if he knew Ross did it. There's no saying his mind is all there. Could be worse off than Dale. We'll see if anyone at the casino remembers him, maybe knows some details of the heist or what happened to him after."

The drive back into Vegas was becoming so familiar to Shane that he recognized certain trees along the road. He was not a big fan of running in circles, but at least Dale had given them a name, and that was something more than just an obnoxious rancher and endless sand.

The Avignon Casino was not on the Strip, but not far away. It wasn't one of the massive resorts like the Wynn or the Bellagio, but it wasn't a hole-in-the-wall, either. It looked like it might have been surviving solely on the business of those who didn't want to endure the sensory overload of the bigger casinos or just wanted to experience some nostalgia. Even the exterior was a little more laid-back and reserved, a sort of cool sixties vibe that made it look like a place for people who wore sunglasses at night and still listened to Sinatra on vinyl.

The interior of the casino matched the outside. Everything had a polished, old-school veneer to it. Shane was surprised that he liked the look of it, though he still preferred the out-of-the-way hotel he'd checked into to begin with. If only someone hadn't tried to kill him there.

The inside of Avignon was more laidback and quieter than the other places they had visited. The volume was not overwhelming, but the crowd size was still decent. Shane scanned the casino from the entrance for ghosts.

Shane circled the room with Ventura at his side. He tried to look casual so no one would be suspicious. He realized searching for a ghost looked a lot like casing a place before a burglary.

Toward the rear of the room, he spotted a ghost near the cashier's cage. The spirit was a young man in a leather jacket and blue jeans, an outfit that looked like it would have been uncomfortable in the desert heat.

Shane nodded to Ventura and made sure the other man saw the ghost and then headed toward the spirit. Aside from deep, almost purple bags under the ghost's eyes, he looked healthy. However he had died had not taken a great physical toll on his appearance.

Initiating a conversation with a person no one else could see in a crowded casino was no easy task. Shane didn't want to draw any more attention to himself than necessary, but he was also very tired of all the running around he and Ventura were doing.

"Hey, what's your name?" Shane asked, standing next to the ghost. The spirit glanced at him and ignored him at first until Shane asked again, locking eyes with the ghost.

Ventura stood on his other side so Shane could look at him when he spoke, giving the impression that he wasn't talking to thin air.

"You're talking to me?" the ghost asked.

"Yeah," Shane said. "Looking for someone who knows about the Emerald."

"I know the Emerald," the ghost said. "What do you want to know about the Emerald?"

"Jack Dallas," Shane answered.

The ghost furrowed his brow. Up close, Shane could see burst capillaries across the ghost's flesh, along his cheeks, and down his neck. A strange chemical smell came from him.

"Who's Jack Dallas?" the ghost asked.

"Ran this place in the sixties," Shane said.

The ghost laughed loudly, and Shane ignored him, still trying to appear casual. No one in the room gave them a second glance.

"The sixties? How old do you think I look, man?" the ghost snickered.

Shane placed a hand on the ghost's shoulder, shutting him up immediately.

"I need to know about Jack Dallas. If you don't know, who does?"

He let his hand slip away, and the ghost stared at him in silence for a long moment.

"How'd you do that?" he asked softly.

"Dallas," Shane repeated.

The ghost shook his head, and the chemical smell thickened.

"I've only been here since the nineties, man. I got some bad stuff from a guy on the Strip, took me on a real bad trip. You want old-old, you gotta go out back. Bags lives by the kitchen dumpsters back there. She's been here forever."

Shane and Ventura left the ghost and made their way to the rear of the casino. Ventura had to flash his badge to get them into the kitchen and then out a side door to the dumpsters lined up at the end of a narrow alley. A cook was leaning against a wall having a cigarette but left quickly with another badge flash.

"Never met a dumpster ghost before," Ventura said when the man was gone.

"Not everyone is discerning about their hangouts after death," Shane said.

He walked down the row of dumpsters, lifting lids and looking between them until he had inspected all of them. There were no ghosts around any of them.

Shane knocked on the last dumpster.

"Someone named Bags out here?" he asked.

There was no response.

"Maybe our guy inside meant some other dumpster," Ventura suggested.

Shane looked at the other man and then cocked his head.

"No, he meant these ones," he said.

The ghost of a woman stood behind Ventura, taller than him by several inches. Blood and vomit covered her from her chin down, caked into a black and white feather-covered costume. More feathers atop her head stretched up several feet like the plumes of a giant bird.

Sparkling jewels were dotted across the bloody bodice of her outfit and through the strange crown holding the feathers atop her head. Bags had been a showgirl. Now, her flesh was as pale as a snake's belly, and her eyes were stark red, leaking blood from the corners like tears.

"What do you need, Ace?" the ghost said, laying her hands on Ventura's shoulders.

Ventura froze. Bags smiled, showing bloody teeth. Her lipstick was smeared up the left side of her face and nearly the same color as the blood in her mouth.

"Ryan," Ventura said, keeping his voice calm.

"You're fine, I think. She's not planning to hurt you," Shane said before looking toward the ghost. "Right?"

The ghost's smile widened, and she leaned forward, letting her hands slip down Ventura's chest and then cross as she embraced him from behind, resting her head on his shoulder.

"Oh no, sweetheart. I'm as gentle as a kitten," she said.

Ventura clenched his jaw, and he stared daggers at Shane. He looked like every muscle in his body had tensed from head to toe. Shane stayed where he was, watching the ghost's hands, but not doing anything she might perceive as threatening.

"Good to know," Shane said. "We were told you might know something about the Emerald, specifically about Jack Dallas."

Bags pursed her lips and rolled her eyes, causing more bloody tears to run down her face.

"Oh, I remember Jackie. What do you want to know about that crook?"

"Not a fan, huh?" Shane said.

Bags ran her hands across Ventura's chest as though appreciating the texture of the fabric.

"Was anyone a fan of Jackie? He stole my tips. He slapped the girls around and bungled I don't know how many high rollers with his big mouth and made them go to other casinos. The man was a plague. I'm glad he got offed."

"He was murdered?" Shane asked. "You know that for sure?"

"Oh yeah. Pete Ciccone and Bava tracked him down after he robbed the count room. Did you know he did that? Took the entire haul, and we had Sinatra in that weekend. Can you believe it? First show outside of the Sands ever. Him and Dean Martin and Joey Bishop and, ya know, those other guys. Frankie gave me a twenty-dollar tip that night."

She squeezed Ventura tightly, pressing her cheek to his as she lost herself in the memory for a moment. Ventura's expression soured considerably.

"But they found him?" Shane asked to get her back on track.

"Of course. Jackie's no criminal genius. I was serving drinks when they came back, and they had to call Mr. Doves. They buried him out there, but they didn't find the money. At least, that's what they told Mr. Doves. You could never tell with Bava. He seemed very untrustworthy."

"Where did they kill him?" Shane asked.

Bags shrugged, causing the feathers on her head to bob and jostle.

"Out near the old Hofstetter Mine. It's where they did all their business, if you know what I mean. Why you boys so curious about Jackie? You looking for his money?"

"Looking for him, actually," Shane said. "His ghost is out there. He's been killing people."

Bags stood up straight then, letting her hands slip back to Ventura's shoulders as she frowned dramatically.

"That son of a bitch came back? That's just like him. He's like bed bugs, always there just ruining everything. This place went to hell after that heist. I hope you find him, and I hope you drop him down a hole where no one will ever find him."

"Definitely plan to do something when we find him," Shane said.

"Good," the ghost said. "If you find him, you tell him I helped you do it. Tell him Janice Bagnoli ratted his thief ass out."

She brushed Ventura's shoulders as though cleaning lint from them and then stepped back, clasping her hands in front of her chest once she released him. He stepped away from her more quickly than he intended, turning to face her as he came to Shane's side.

"I'll be sure to let him know," Shane said. "You've been very helpful, Janice."

"Any time, Ace," she said, blood dripping from her wide, enthusiastic smile as she winked at them.

CHAPTER 18
A DEAD MAN IN THE DESERT

Ventura was eager to leave the casino, setting a swift pace as he led Shane back out to the car.

"You could have given me a hand back there," he said as he got behind the wheel.

"She was harmless," Shane dismissed.

"You didn't know that. She smelled like old meat."

"Ghosts smell; I don't know what to tell you. She gave us the mine, that's good. We just need to locate it."

"Already did. Take a guess," Ventura held up the map on his phone. A pin was placed right on the edge of Ross' property.

"That tracks. Ross has to know about him, but he's not keeping Dallas caged like the others. I'm guessing that's where your mob guys fit in," Shane said.

"Yeah," Ventura agreed, leaving the lot, and hitting the road. "I need to talk to someone at the Vegas field office about these Philly guys in town. See who's here and if anyone is keeping track."

"They have to be after the money, right? Talking to Ross because he's got a bead on it from Dallas."

"Maybe," Ventura said. "Not sure why Ross wouldn't just keep it for himself."

"He's selling Dallas," Shane guessed. "That's why the Endless Night is here. Dallas is famous, right? Vaguely, I guess. Mobster who stole from his casino and vanished, according to legend. That's a top-shelf prize for an Endless Night collector."

"Could be giving the money to the Philly outfit to curry favor. Showing he's trustworthy. Maybe they're going into business," Ventura said, furthering the speculation.

They were heading back down the Strip toward the Grand as they talked.

"Whatever's going on, Ross has to be involved, so I need to see if I can get a favor. I'll drop you back at the hotel and pick you up later if I find something out," Ventura said.

"Thanks, Dad," Shane replied.

They pulled up in front of the doors, and Shane got out.

"If I'm not here when you get back, it's because I went somewhere else," he said.

"Sure," Ventura replied. "Don't get killed."

"I haven't yet."

Shane banged his palm on the roof of the car and stepped back to let the other man leave. He had no intention of waiting in the room for Ventura to do homework with the Las Vegas team. He had enough information to go on to make some headway. No more aimless wandering: They had a target.

Shane understood that Ventura still wanted to do things by the book, but that was his book. He was concerned with Ross and the mob guys from Philadelphia. Shane didn't care about them one way or the other, though he planned to let Ross know what he thought about sending two gunmen after him.

The real target was Dallas. They had a good lead on where he was, and where his haunted item was waiting. That meant a good chance to end him and maybe find those missing people. Shane had no doubt they were dead, but they deserved the closure of having Dallas stopped for good.

Shane's car was still at the Golden Gate Towers. He walked back to the hotel, stopping along the way to get new cigarettes as he wrestled with the puzzle of Dallas and Ross' relationship. He and Ventura had devised a plausible enough explanation for everything that was happening except for the murders. Why was Ross letting Dallas run free?

Shane didn't like holes in theories, and Dallas' murders was a big hole. If Ross had Dallas in his possession to sell him, he could have kept him caged. If he didn't have him in hand, why didn't Dallas kill Ross? The only way he'd get answers was to confront Dallas firsthand.

Ventura could worry about red tape or operating within the law as much as he wanted. Shane planned to find the mine Bags had told them about now that he knew where to look.

The gambling ghosts were back in the parking lot when he returned to his car. They ignored him as much as they ever had despite seeming somewhat surprised to see him alive when he returned to his car. Not surprised enough to stop their game, but the dealer offered him a half-hearted wave as he pulled out of the lot.

Shane left the city and headed back into the desert. By now, he knew the way far too well. It was like he was just commuting to work at this point, following the same old path he'd traveled so many times.

It was late, but Dale had mentioned that Dallas didn't like coming out in the light. Shane felt like he'd have better success in the dark.

He saw where the mine was located on Ventura's map, not far from the canyon where they had discovered the dead body and the ghost. From the ridge above, looking down into the valley that occupied much of Ross' ranch, he hadn't seen anything that looked like a mine entrance. That didn't mean one wasn't there. Ross clearly liked his privacy and had gone out of his way to keep things hidden from outside view.

Shane drove wide and away from Ross' property to ensure that the rancher or any other associates he might have with him wouldn't see Shane coming. He left the road and traveled through the desert, stopping next to the cover of the same rocks that Ventura had used on their previous visit.

He left the car and retraced the steps he had taken, shadowing Ross' property line as he made his way toward the spot where he believed the mine entrance to be. The wind had died down some since they had seen Dale at his trailer, but not by much. Sand and grit still blasted against him as he walked, creating a faint rustling sound as a backdrop to his travels.

A new sound joined the white noise of blowing sand as Shane got closer to the mine. There were a few quick yips at first, and then faint growling as he moved in to investigate. A short distance away, huddled near the trunks of some stumpy, gnarled trees close to the ridge above another canyon, Shane saw a group of three coyotes digging at the ground and fighting each other as they tried to pull something free.

The largest coyote pushed between the two others and sunk its head into a hole they'd dug. Shane watched it bear down then brace itself and pull, dragging a human arm out of the sand.

Shane picked up a rock and tossed it at the tree, hitting it with a loud smacking sound before it landed next to the wild dogs, startling the trio. He came toward them and they turned on him quickly, growling and showing teeth to guard their prize.

Another rock hit the tree and Shane yelled, pulling out his lighter and sparking it to life as he waved it around. The coyotes growled and backed up, refusing to flee what they saw as a convenient meal.

Shane kicked sand and more rocks their way, yelling, and swinging the lighter as he waved his hands, looking as intimidating as he could. Coyotes were opportunists at best and were usually not keen on confrontation. They also didn't look like they were starving and desperate.

The smallest one backed off, and Shane kicked a spray of sand after it. The debris peppered the other two, forcing them back, and then, with another yell, all three retreated, leaving Shane to claim their prize.

He knew they wouldn't stray far, but he wanted to see what they'd found. Moving quickly, Shane came to the shallow hole near the tree and knelt, using the Zippo to illuminate the area.

The grave was shallow, as the others had been, but the body inside was only a few hours old at most. It was a woman, maybe in her thirties, dressed for hiking with well-worn boots and a backpack still strapped to her back. Her blonde hair was tied back but saturated with blood that came from the wound in her head. Another hole like the last two victims, frostbitten along the edges.

Shane could see no other wounds on the body with a perfunctory inspection. It didn't matter, of course. She was dead and Dallas had done it, another victim to add to the tally.

Shane thought the wound on her head would have looked like a gunshot to someone not incredibly skilled in gunshot wounds. Ventura was right, though. It was not from a gun, it was a hole poked through the woman's skull. The ghost had killed her with a finger, Shane guessed, pushed right through her skull and into her brain.

"Now who the hell do you think you are playing around in my sandbox, Chrome Dome?"

"Chrome Dome?" Shane turned toward the source of the voice. "You really are from the sixties, huh?"

The ghost stood behind him in the dark, his feet invisible in the shadows. He was slightly shorter than Shane and wore a plum-colored suit with a loose black tie. His hair was swept back and held up with what would have been product when he was alive, but now was just smeared with blood from two bullet holes in his forehead.

"I don't like people sniffing around in my business. Makes me think you're looking for something," the ghost continued.

"Sounds like you're paranoid," Shane replied.

He was still crouched next to the corpse. Dallas was close enough to attack and catch Shane at a disadvantage in his awkward position.

"Does this look paranoid?" The ghost pointed to the holes in his head.

He turned to one side, and Shane saw that the back of the ghost's skull had been blown wide open, exposing brain and blood within.

"That a typical mob hit back in the day? Only seen it in movies," Shane said. He wondered why they bothered to shoot the second bullet.

"You're that guy." Dallas ignored the question. "The bald guy who killed Patches."

"Patches? Not sure I ever had the pleasure," Shane replied.

Dallas shook his head, half a scowl on his face as he shook his finger at Shane.

"No, Ross said a Fed and a bald guy done in his little guard dog. I thought he was blowing smoke, but here you are, seeing me clear as day. What's your trick, Chrome Dome? You some kind of ghost killer?"

Shane slowly got to his feet, his hands at his sides where the ghost could see them. Dallas didn't move to stop him. He was more wrapped up in learning more about Shane.

"Patches was the burned ghost on Ross' ranch?" Shane said. "Yeah, I had to put that one down. He shouldn't have run."

"Shouldn't have run," Dallas repeated mockingly. "You sound like a tough guy. Look like a tough guy, too. Bet you haven't been put in your place in a long time, huh?"

"Not as long as you'd think," Shane told him.

Dallas scoffed.

"Well, doesn't look like anyone's put *you* down yet. Maybe I can oblige."

"Maybe," Shane said. "Or maybe you just talk a lot. Maybe you should stay here running your mouth while I go find your money."

"That's my goddamn money. I earned it!" Dallas snapped.

"I heard you stole it and ran like a coward," Shane told him. "Janice Bagnoli says 'Hi,' by the way."

Dallas sneered. His body surged forward and came at Shane in a fury, snarling as he reached out. Shane let him come, raising a fist, and clocking the ghost with a right hook to his jaw.

The ghost growled, more from surprise than anything else, and was knocked down. He stared up at Shane with a wide-eyed rage as he reset his slightly crooked jaw.

"Who the hell are you?" the ghost demanded.

"I'm the bald guy who's going to rip your head from your shoulders."

CHAPTER 19:
ENTOMBED

Dallas growled again and leapt at Shane though there was no movement below the spirit's waist. He was ensconced in shadow and moved with it as though it was a part of him.

Shane caught him as Dallas reached for his throat, intent on strangling him. They grappled, and Shane managed a few shots into the ghost's gut and rib cage.

Dallas fought like a man rather than a ghost, and not a very skilled one. For all his tough talk, he was not much of a fighter. Shane guessed he had people to do his fighting for him back in the day. What he had going for him was anger and power. When he resisted Shane or struck him back, he was strong.

Shane got in another blow to the ghost's face, this time knocking out one of his front teeth. Dallas scrambled back, reaching for his face, and touching the gap where the tooth had been. His eyes were wide with shock, realizing for the first time that Shane was causing permanent damage.

Instead of attacking him again, the ghost took a step back. Shane's hands were still balled into fists, ready to take Dallas on, but the darkness swallowed him. Shane stood still, scanning the night. The ghost had vanished, absorbed into the shadows around him.

"You're a sneaky one." Dallas' voice came from several directions at once. Shane tensed, putting his back to the tree next to the dead body.

"Look who's talking," he replied.

"Maybe I'll take my time with you. Peel that bald head off your skull like a grape, see what's inside," Dallas whispered.

He sounded closer that time and Shane turned, leaving the tree for more open ground. There was nothing to see in any direction.

The cold air was his only warning, carried on the dry, warmer wind still blowing across the desert. Shane felt it and turned swiftly, catching the ghost as he tried to attack from behind and throwing him to the ground with his own momentum.

Dallas swore as he hit the ground, half-hidden in darkness, and glared up at Shane.

"I'm getting tired of you wasting my time," the ghost said.

"We've been at this for less than five minutes," Shane said. "You need a nap or something?"

Dallas rushed again, low to the ground like one of the coyotes, almost camouflaged in shadow.

Shane kicked the ghost in the face, his foot hitting Dallas in the nose with a crunch. The ghost fell backward, his nose plastered to the side of his face and broken.

"If you want me to stop beating you senseless, tell me why Ross doesn't have you caged like the others."

"I'm going to gut you like a pig while you're still screaming," Dallas said.

He came at Shane again, and this time, Shane's foot hit the other side of the ghost's face, dislocating his jaw in the opposite direction of the first one. Dallas quickly sank back into the shadows.

"Ross lets you have a real long leash, huh?" Shane said, watching for movement.

"Ross doesn't tell me what to do," Dallas growled from nearby. "He does what I say. If he wants to see a dime of that money, he'll remember his place."

"Why would Bennett Ross trust a bloated failure like you?" Shane asked.

"Failure?" the ghost hissed. "I took the Emerald from a two-bit sawdust joint with watered-down drinks to the best goddamn spot in Vegas. I negotiated the deal for Sinatra. That was me! Not Joey Doves, me!"

He came at Shane again, lurching from the shadows at his feet and pulling him to the ground. Shane landed on his face as Dallas crawled up his back, digging into him with fingers like ice picks. When the spirit made it halfway up his back, Shane threw an elbow and cracked his jaw a third time, knocking him to one side and giving Shane the chance to get on his knees and grasp Dallas' head in his hands.

Dallas brought a knee into Shane's groin, and Shane lost his grip. They rolled together, Shane keeping the ghost from digging his fingers into his flesh again by keeping him off-balance. They were getting closer to the canyon's edge, and in the dark, Shane could not tell how far up they were.

"The coyotes are going to eat your goddamn face off, you know that?" Dallas forced Shane onto his back and pinned him by the wrists.

The wind had picked up, howling along the canyon below them, and pelting Shane with more stinging debris. The ghost was straddling him, leaning in close to gloat. Shane could see the stars and the edge of the crescent moon beyond Dallas' head, but the ghost was right there, looming in his face, blocking everything. He was too close.

Shane didn't reply. Instead, he leaned forward, closing the gap between them, and sank his teeth into the ghost's throat. Dallas screamed in surprise as Shane bit, shearing through spongy, unliving flesh that froze his teeth and sent shocks of pain through the nerve endings.

Dallas recoiled, but Shane was embedded deeply. He grabbed the ghost's wrists as he pulled back and then forced his jaws to close, taking a massive bite out of the spirit's neck.

The ghost bucked, and Shane was ready to continue the fight when he felt the ground beneath him shift. They were too close to the canyon edge, he realized, balanced on unstable rock.

The panicked look on the ghost's face quickly turned to one of perverse amusement.

"Enjoy the trip."

The words faded with the ghost. Dallas was gone in a blink, sucked into the darkness. Shane jerked, no longer holding the tension of the retreating ghost's arms as he popped from existence. The sudden shift caused an abrupt spasm, and Shane felt the stone give way beneath him.

He tried to roll away, to scramble back to stable ground, but the chunk of stone he was on was too large. The canyon ridge crumbled into the darkness, and Shane fell with it.

The sky pulled away, the stars and the moon vanishing just like Dallas had. Darkness replaced it all, and it happened so fast. Shane felt his back slam hard against the stone, and his head struck something that caused his vision to flash white. His head felt like it was being pushed apart from the inside even as a searing heat ran up his leg.

He couldn't remember where he was; there was only the pain and the spinning in his head.

The world didn't stop moving until, blissfully, everything was swallowed by the same darkness as the sky.

✳ ✳ ✳

Shane awoke with a cry of pain. A small animal scuttled away, stepping on his face as it went, and he reached for his head. It had chewed on the side of his face, eating the flesh of the open wound there.

The sky above was a clear blue and patched with clouds framed by looming canyon walls on either side. His head hurt beyond words, and so did his leg. He tried to see where he was and what was happening, but fire shot through his skull at the simplest movement.

Shane hissed, clenching his teeth, and held still for a moment to acclimate. He slipped his fingers behind his head and felt the back of his head. Cool, tacky blood met his touch, but his skull was intact as near as he could tell. A concussion, maybe, but nothing life-threatening. At least not on his head.

Shane looked down, the effort making him wince, and stared at his leg, or as much of it as he could see. His left leg, from halfway down his thigh, was hidden from view beneath a slab of stone. He tried to pull it free, but it would not budge. The rock had pinned him. The pain was bearable, not even intense, but he might as well have been shackled in place for all the range of motion it afforded him.

"Of course," he muttered.

The air was stifling hot from the desert sun. He was out of the direct light, but that would only last until midday. Once the sun was overhead, he would bake in it if he could not find a way out.

Shane took some deep breaths and leaned forward. He could just reach the edges of the rock over his leg, but he had only the weakest grip. He was caught at a poor angle that gave him no leverage to move the slab.

His right leg was not pinned and only partially under the cover of the fallen stone that held him in place. He could not pull his leg back far enough to use it to push, but he could kick and dig at the ground below, using his heel to scratch at the sandy canyon floor. It, too was mostly rock. There was no way he could scrape through it with a boot and free his other leg.

A shadow passed across his face. Shane looked up in time to see a bird land on the canyon's edge, staring at him over a curved beak. A buzzard, drawn by the sight and smell of blood. He swore at it, but it stayed put, watching him. Waiting for him to fall asleep or die, something that would allow it to swoop in for a quick meal.

The minutes ticked by. Shane's smashed phone was as useless as the rocks around him. He had no way to alert Ventura. And Dallas was probably still watching somewhere out there. Maybe Ross already knew about him.

Shane had no way to know how much blood he'd lost but with an injury, in the desert heat, his timeline was short. He could die of dehydration in a day under those conditions. That was likely why Dallas had not finished him off. The ghost would have thought a drawn-out death was more punishing. He wasn't wrong.

The direct sunlight crept down the canyon wall until it was on the rock covering Shane's leg. He could feel it getting hotter against his flesh, and soon, the sun was shining right in his eyes.

Something skittered in the rocks, and Shane saw a flash of movement. He stayed still, focusing on what he had seen until a thin brown and gray body crept out into view. A rat, lean but still healthy, watched him with black eyes. It stood on its hind legs, sniffed the air, and turned toward the stone on Shane's leg.

"Like hell you're eating my leg," he muttered, grabbing a nearby rock.

Shane threw the rock, missing the rat but scaring it away. Above him, two buzzards joined the first at the canyon ledge. The Mojave was waiting to devour him.

The sun continued to climb until it was directly over Shane. Even with his eyes closed, all he saw was blinding red. It made his headache worse, and the pain increased by the minute. He had to drape one arm over his eyes and sneak peeks only occasionally to make sure the rats and birds weren't coming for him.

He felt the skin of his forearm burning in the sun, but it was better than his face. He kept his eyes covered until he heard a faint sniffing sound much closer than he would have liked.

Shane pulled his arm away and was met with a stunned growl. A coyote, either one from last night or a new straggler, was only inches away, smelling the blood on the rock beside his head. It snarled when he moved, and he quickly grabbed a nearby rock, hurling it toward the animal. The coyote yelped when the projectile hit it in the chest and forced it to scuttle away.

More rocks followed as Shane pelted the wild dog and yelled at it to go away until it got the message and vanished. He didn't think it would stay away long, and it might not come back alone.

He heard something approaching again just minutes later, a faint scratching and moaning sound preceding the appearance of something new. Not a coyote this time, but a man. What had once been a man but had not been in a long time.

The ghost was massively decayed, one of the worst Shane had seen. Flesh had dried and rotted across its body. Its clothing was ragged, torn scraps that hung haphazardly from its neck and across its shoulders and wrists.

Shane had to rethink his initial thought that the ghost was male as there was no way to tell anymore. With most of the face and body rotted away, it was little more than a skeleton covered in leather and jerky.

Some of the exposed bones were cracked and splintered, bearing signs of teeth marks from animals that had gnawed on the body. Whoever the ghost had been, it, too, had died in the desert and had been consumed by the things that lived there.

The ghost still had one eye. The left one was sunken into a leathery eye socket. It was milk-white and encrusted with yellow and brown sludge around the edges, but it still moved and focused on Shane.

It walked slowly, shuffling on legs made of bone wrapped in shreds of rotted denim. The ghost must have heard Shane yelling from wherever it had been and come wandering to find him.

Lipless jaws parted, and a sound came out of the ghost's mouth. Shane thought it must have been speaking, but it was impossible to tell. Instead of words, it produced a dry rasp, something closer to the hiss of a snake than any human language.

The ghost extended a hand, its skeletal fingers tipped with black, filth-encrusted nails, and came toward him.

CHAPTER 20
THE WALKING DEAD

Shane had no way to escape. The ghost was slow and stiff, and it lacked coordination, but it was free to move. Shane was on his back and could only move from the waist up.

Instead of coming for his head, the ghost shambled toward the trapped leg. Shane struggled, trying to pull free but making no more progress than he had for the entire morning. He was weak and thirsty, and he lacked the strength or ability to put up a serious fight.

The ghost looked at him, its rotted eye fixed on his, and rasped again as it leaned down. The skeletal hands gripped the stone, and in a surprisingly swift and smooth motion, it lifted the slab and flipped it back against the canyon wall.

Shane stayed motionless for a moment, and the ghost stepped back, rasping once more. Shane cautiously pulled in his leg, fighting the numbness of the pins-and-needles sensation that took over now that he was free and the pressure had been lifted.

The rotted ghost did nothing as Shane took time to unsteadily get to his feet. He leaned against the canyon wall, balanced on his other leg, while he fought the painful sensation of the circulation returning to the leg.

"Thank you for that," Shane said, watching the ghost.

The spirit replied hoarsely, another unintelligible word, and then nodded slowly.

"I take it you've been here a while," Shane said.

The spirit shook its head and ambled closer. Its movements were still slow, but Shane saw it was more badly injured than he thought. The flesh he had at first assumed was dried by the desert was severely burned by something far worse than the sun and desert heat.

"These burns are strange." Shane looked at the few patches where enough flesh covered bone.

He had seen people burned in fires, and by acid and chemicals and even oil. The ghost's burns were warped, almost patterned, with ridges and sections that didn't make sense.

The ghost nodded and pointed somewhere to the northwest.

"Faaaarrr," it rasped, barely capable of producing the word.

"It happened far from here?" Shane asked.

The ghost nodded as Shane tried out his leg, balancing awkwardly. It could hold his weight, and that was what he needed it to do.

"Do you know the way out of here?" he asked.

The ghost nodded and pointed ahead. Shane started walking, limping on his leg, and the ghost hobbled along beside him.

"What happened to you?" Shane asked.

The ghost's throat rumbled like gravel rattling in a can.

"Alllll… brrrrrnnnnddd."

"All burned," Shane repeated, and the ghost nodded. "More people were burned?"

"Alllllll… saaaammmmme."

"All… same?" Shane asked. Again, the ghost nodded. "A lot of people burned at the same time?"

The ghost shook its head, and Shane grunted.

"Burned the same way?" he tried. This time, the ghost nodded.

"A lot of people burned the same way, but not the same time, far from here."

"Caaannnnnt eeee eeeeeeen," the ghost continued.

They continued down the narrow canyon, the sun blazing onto Shane's head and back, as he puzzled over the words' meaning.

"Can't be seen," he said at last.

The ghost nodded. Shane wasn't sure what the statement meant.

"How did you get here if it happened far away?" Shane asked.

The ghost pointed at the canyon wall to the west.

"Taaaakkkkknnnn," it rasped.

"You were taken," Shane translated. "To the ranch?"

The ghost nodded, and Shane grunted. Ross had stolen the ghost from someplace. He wasn't surprised. His spirit collection was not just made up of locals. The sheer number implied he'd been hunting them elsewhere and then, presumably, selling them to the Endless Night stragglers or whoever had a hankering for a ghost collection.

"How come he doesn't have you penned up like the others? He make a deal with you?" Shane asked.

Dallas had dangled his treasure over Ross' head and seemed to have negotiated his freedom with it. But Dallas was also a killer. This burned ghost was far too polite to be doing business with Bennett Ross.

"Caannttt," the ghost answered.

"He can't? Why?"

"Aaaaangrrrrssss," it told him, the awkward word sounding more like a throat clearing than anything.

"Dangerous?"

The ghost nodded.

"It's too dangerous for you to be with the other ghosts?"

As horrifying as the spirit looked, it wasn't projecting dangerous vibes. Certainly not ones that put other ghosts at risk.

The ghost nodded again but didn't offer a better explanation. The canyon walls on either side began to recede as the path forward cleared, and the ghost led Shane back out into the open desert.

Shane limped on, but the ghost remained at the edge of the canyon, refusing to travel farther.

"End of the road for you?" Shane asked, turning back.

The ghost nodded again and pointed toward some rocks not far off.

"Caaarrr," it croaked.

"Thank you for your help," Shane told it. The ghost didn't reply, watching in silence as he limped onward toward the rocks. His surroundings became familiar in time, and he picked out the path he'd traveled the night before.

Shane returned to his car, getting inside, and rolling down the windows. There was no water in the car, but a breeze picked up once he was on the road and driving away from the desert. It was better than nothing.

His leg hurt, but he didn't think the injury was bad. The bone wasn't broken. It might be bruised at worst, but the head wound was a problem.

Once he was in the city, Shane followed street signs until he found a hospital. Thanks to his bloody head wound, he was immediately taken to see a doctor in the ER. They cleaned the wound and performed some tests before letting him know he had a concussion, some minor bruising, and was suffering from dehydration.

By the time he checked out against medical advice, it was late afternoon. Most of the day had been wasted trapped under a rock. He wondered how Ventura had fared on his side of things and drove back to the hotel.

"Jesus, Ryan, what the hell happened?" the agent asked when he returned to their shared room. Ventura was at a desk, using his computer next to a half-eaten burger when Shane entered.

"Met Dallas." Shane grabbed a bottle of water from the minibar. The hospital had given him fluids, but he still felt dry. "Got stuck under a rock for the better part of a day."

"You met him?" Ventura asked.

"He tried to kill me but opted to let the desert do it. He's holding the cash over Ross. That's why he's not imprisoned with the others. Sounds like they worked a deal, but I don't know the terms. You have any luck?"

"What happened to your head?" Ventura asked, ignoring the question.

"Told you. Stuck under a rock. You?"

"The FBI knows about the Philadelphia outfit in town but hasn't seen anything to raise red flags. I couldn't tell them what I know, so the bureau has nothing to do with them or Ross right now. Dead end, basically."

Shane sighed and grabbed the rest of Ventura's hamburger, taking a bite before continuing.

"I met someone in the desert," he explained. "Ghost that was burned to hell, way worse than the one on Ross' ranch."

"Another one of his guards?" Ventura asked.

Shane shook his head and explained what happened.

"He said he was taken from a place with a lot of burned people who weren't all burned at the same time. What's that sound like to you?"

Ventura shook his head, confusion clear on his face.

"No idea. Crematorium, maybe?" he asked.

"I thought that for a second, but these burns weren't normal. Plus, he pointed to the northwest. I think those burns were radiation burns."

"You're thinking the Nevada Test Site," Ventura said. "Where they did all those nuclear tests."

"The ghost said it was too dangerous for him to be kept with the others. That didn't make sense at first, but then I thought what if he didn't mean he's too dangerous, but that his haunted item is too dangerous? Like it's radioactive."

"They did nearly a thousand nuclear tests out there for the better part of forty years. It's possible. It'd also be a hell of a coverup if there were civilians out there who died from radiation exposure," Ventura said. "I don't understand what this has to do with Dallas, though."

"Maybe nothing," Shane admitted. "But Dallas is new in the area, right? Bags said he was killed in that mine on the property. If he only resurfaced now, Ross is probably just getting into this business. His guys are harvesting ghosts from the test site out west, and he needs to store them somewhere safe. He's keeping them underground, but the more dangerous ones are separate, not for the sake of the ghosts but for himself. Maybe they opened the mine to store these radioactive ghosts and let Dallas out in the process."

"So, he stumbled into a homicidal ghost with a three-million-dollar payday," Ventura said.

"Ross is a parasite just sucking the blood from whatever he can. The mob, the Endless Night, he's going all-in on everything. He gets a cushy deal with some East Coast crime syndicate, he gets set up as a supplier for the cult, and he has an inside track on rare, radioactive ghosts," Shane said.

"You can't just walk into the Nevada Test Site or Yucca Flat, though," Ventura said. "That whole area is tightly regulated. I know someone who works at Nellis Air Force Base and oversaw the test and training range. It's not just a public park. Area 51 is over there."

"Most people probably can't," Shane agreed. "But if we're right, people died in those tests. Those were supposed to *just* be tests, so if someone like Ross knows where those bodies are buried, maybe he has some off-the-books help on the inside."

Shane finished the burger, and Ventura leaned back in his chair, exhaling loudly.

"You're talking about a pretty serious coverup. As conspiracies go, this one is up there. Saying people were intentionally exposed to the blast tests and their bodies were left in the desert is not just an obscure piece of Americana."

"No," Shane said. "Might not even be that insidious. Maybe they weren't all intentional. Maybe they were accidents, and some people were in the wrong place at the wrong time. Whatever happened, Ross seems to know about it, and it's supplying him with ghosts he's selling to restart the Endless Night. That can't happen."

"So, what do you want to do now?" Ventura asked.

"You said you have a friend at the Air Force base. Maybe we should take a tour," Shane suggested.

"I have an acquaintance," Ventura corrected. "And I haven't spoken to him in years. And asking to be allowed into a secure government site for reasons you can't explain is a hell of a way to reconnect with someone."

"You'll think of something," Shane said. "Let's go before it gets too late."

"There's absolutely no way this will work for us," Ventura said.

Nevertheless, he stood up and put on his jacket.

CHAPTER 21

DEAD-END DRIVE

"What the hell are you even asking me?"

Ventura rubbed his brow, trying to stay calm and not come across as awkward as he felt. Shane stood a few paces away, his head covered by a partially blood-stained bandage and his arms folded across his chest.

"Just wanted to see if we could get a look at the old test site where the bombs were dropped," he explained again.

Ventura's acquaintance was Colonel Perry Halbrecht, and however Ventura knew the man, they were not friends. Shane wondered if they had maybe worked in an office for a few months and Ventura had grossly overestimated how much the other man liked him.

"Why would I do that? Why would you want to do that? That's a former nuclear test site, Xander. As in radioactive material. No one just goes out there. Now, if you want a proper tour, you can schedule one of those through the Department of Energy website. I think they're booking a year in advance."

"I see," Ventura said.

Colonel Halbrecht was seated behind his desk in a sparsely decorated office. He wore his dress blues, and Shane thought they must have just caught him coming from or going to a more important meeting.

"You should see. The Department of Energy and the NNSA have been overseeing that site for years, and I can assure you, people don't just go there to look around."

Ventura offered one final less-than-convincing plea for a good word on his behalf and Colonel Halbrecht shot it down quickly, thanking the agent for wasting his time, and telling him to leave.

"That was embarrassing," Shane said as they crossed the base back to Ventura's car.

"Told you it wouldn't work," the other man said. "But it was still useful."

"In what way? That man just talked to you like you were a child."

"Yeah, he did. I once watched him chug two liters of peach wine cooler and then immediately vomit it across his grandmother's back patio on Lake Erie. He doesn't talk like that. Not to me, anyway. He went very serious the moment I told him where we wanted to go."

They got back into the car, and Ventura glanced in the rearview mirror.

"You think he knows something's up out there? Maybe someone stealing ghosts?"

"Not that detailed." Ventura shook his head. "Doubt he knows anything about ghosts. And the test site is, what, a thousand square miles? Fifteen hundred? That's a lot of desolate ground for someone like Ross to cover, and I didn't specify a spot. I don't think he knows who is doing it or what they're doing, but he knows something is happening out there. And me asking about it set him on the defense."

"So, we're not getting a military assist. But if there are radioactive ghosts, there are other ways to prove it," Shane said. "Hiding radiation isn't as easy as just putting a glowing skeleton in a mine in your backyard."

"No, it isn't," Ventura agreed. "We can track them with something like a Geiger counter. Find your friendly ghost and maybe Dallas at the same time."

"Plus, Ross' secret stash," Shane said. "You know where we can find a Geiger counter around here?"

"We're sixty miles from where they used to drop nuclear bombs. You can find Geiger counters at Walmart."

They left the Air Force base, and Ventura drove them across the city.

Shane had thought he was being sarcastic about Walmart having radiation detectors, but the North Las Vegas Walmart Supercenter proved him wrong when they picked up a pair of digital radiation detectors for less than thirty dollars apiece.

"Ready for another trip to the desert?" Ventura asked.

Shane was truly tired of traveling to Ross' ranch, but at least now, they had an angle and a chance to find what they were looking for. He wanted to bounce Ross' head off a cactus once or twice for wasting so much of their time, though.

Readings from the meters they purchased increased as they approached the ranch, taking the same path to the east of the property and out of sight from the main house where Shane had met Dallas the night before.

Ventura parked at the same spot Shane had previously, and both men left the vehicle. The counts on the meters increased as they got closer to the property, though there was still nothing to see from the ridge. There were ghosts in the cages again, but no signs of Ross or any other living soul.

At the bottom of the ridge along Ross' fence line, Ventura checked the reading on the meter one more time.

"That look dangerous to you?" he asked, turning the meter toward Shane. A display of numbers was present, highlighted in red.

"Do you know how to read that?" he asked.

Ventura shrugged, pulling out his phone.

"Not really. But it's in red, and the guide on the back says that's dangerous."

He turned the meter off and dialed his phone.

"Agent Burke, please. This is Xander Ventura," he said before going silent. Shane waited quietly by his side.

"Burke, it's Ventura. I'm out at Bennett Ross' ranch. Got a call from a friend back east when he heard I was out here about Ross being involved with trafficking some nuclear material. Told him I wasn't working, but since I stopped to check out those murders in the area, I figured I could at least look into it. I got a radiation meter that's spiking like crazy. I think this guy's putting together a dirty bomb on his property, and we are on a clock."

There was another pause while Ventura stared at Shane.

"Absolutely. See you soon."

He hung up the phone and slipped it back into his pocket.

"They're going to raid this place in about a half-hour, and—" he stopped, looking at his phone. "Huh."

"What?" Shane asked.

"Phone died. Had almost a full battery just a second ago."

"Check the counter," Shane said, looking around them.

"Dead, too," Ventura confirmed.

"It's Dallas," Shane said.

"We should—"

Ventura's legs were pulled out from under him, and his sentence cut off as he fell face-first to the ground. Shadows yanked him away from the fence and back toward the ridge as he struggled to free himself.

He grabbed at random scrub and latched onto a rock, holding in place and stopping the ghost from dragging him farther.

Shane ran toward them, his pace slowed by the limp in his leg. The shadow swarmed across Ventura's back, and Dallas rose out of it, grabbing Ventura by the neck and lifting him off the ground as he fully materialized, save for his hidden feet in the darkness.

The ghost held Ventura up, his feet dangling inches from the ground. The agent struggled to pull the hands choking him free but could not even touch them.

"Aren't you supposed to be dead?" Dallas said after seeing Shane.

The ghost thrust Ventura to the side, and the man hit the fence hard, his head cracking against one of the support posts before he crumpled to the dry, desert ground.

"Looks like I'm not," Shane replied.

He dove at the ghost's waist, but Dallas was already gone. The shadows he'd grown from vanished, too, slipping like an oil slick beneath the fence and onto Ross' property before fading from view.

Shane went to Ventura's side, helping the other man sit up as he rubbed his throat.

"What an asshole," the agent said hoarsely.

"Yeah, he is. I think he's underground, below Ross' place. The mine must extend all the way to the house."

Ventura got to his feet, dusting himself off and gingerly checking the back of his head where he hit the fence.

"Didn't even break skin," Shane said. "I think he likes you."

"I bet," Ventura said. "If we're going to get him, we have to do it now. Ross is going to be shut down in no time, and anything radioactive he has on-site will be confiscated."

"We're breaking and entering?" Shane asked. "You sure about that?"

"We got probable cause," Ventura countered. "Come on."

They scaled the fence into Ross' yard. The moment Shane's feet hit the ground, flood lights clicked on along the house and barn. An electronic buzzing filled the air, and the doors to the ghost cages swung open.

Shane cursed and made a beeline for the stables. Ross had upgraded his security since the last time they had been on his property.

The ghosts swarmed out of their cells as the back door of the ranch house opened and a man with a rifle stepped out. His first shot hit the ground to Shane's right. A shot from a second gunman hit the stables ahead of him as he and Ventura ducked and weaved, running for cover.

Shane hit the ground well below the open windows that lined the stable walls and the top half of the door where he would have been visible. Ventura hit the ground with him, crawling through loose hay and dirt toward an open pen full of tools and leather strapping.

Several ghosts entered the stables with them, disturbing the handful of horses Ross kept there. Most of the ghosts passed through without giving the men a second glance, but others were not so quick to ignore them.

Shane watched as the ghost Ventura had identified on their first visit, the mobster Mario Langella, drifted through the hay toward them. His crooked nose made the scowl on his face more intimidating, and his eyes were locked on Ventura.

"Well, look who it is," the ghost said softly.

He rushed for Ventura, but Shane cut the ghost off, catching the dead man's wrist and pulling him to the ground so they were on the same level. A second ghost joined Langella, and soon, a third.

Shane's punch stunned Langella long enough for Shane to trip up the second ghost and get on top of it, smashing the spirit's face into the dirt. Ventura was on his feet behind him. He pulled a pair of ancient-looking horseshoes off the wall and hurled one at the third ghost. The iron forced it away, but more spirits followed.

Ventura threw more horseshoes as Shane fought off those who got too close. Another gunshot caused both men to flatten to the ground. The wood splintered on a support post over Shane's head as the bullet tore through it.

"You have any secret weapons, now's the time," Ventura shouted, swinging a horseshoe into Langella's head and banishing the spirit.

"Don't think we need them." Shane took a swing at another ghost who vanished before he made contact. What had seconds earlier been a swarm of escaping spirits was reduced to a trickle and then, as quickly as they had appeared, they were gone. Inside the stables and outside, every ghost had vanished.

"They're packing up," Shane said. "That was just a distraction to give them a few minutes."

"Packing up the ghosts?" Ventura said. Shane scrambled to the stable wall and stood enough to peer out the nearest window.

"Yeah. Probably have them boxed up Endless Night style. Close the lid, and they're ready for travel."

He looked into the yard for the gunmen who had shot at them. The cages were still open, as was the back door to the ranch house. Shane saw a man's body on the ground next to the door, a rifle at his side, and a spray of blood up the white wall behind him. The escaping ghosts did not discriminate who they killed.

There was no sign of the second gunman. Shane stayed where he was, half-crouched and peering from the window until he cautiously stood. Still concealed by the wall, he grabbed a pitchfork from the tools next to him. He thrust the head of the fork into a pile of hay and picked up a mass before lifting it and pushing it into view of the yard.

No gunshot rang out. Shane threw the pitchfork aside and took a deep breath. He leaned forward and looked out of the window. No one was there.

"Clear," he said to Ventura.

Shane opened the door and headed into the yard. There was little time left to find Jack Dallas before the FBI arrived, and Shane had no intention of letting the ghost survive that long.

Chapter 22

In the Darkness Below

Shane's shoulder was against the wall. He stared at Ventura on the other side of the door frame. The other man nodded, his gun drawn and at the ready. Shane nodded back and then moved swiftly, heading into the house through the open door.

The room was empty of ghosts or people. A hutch on the far wall displayed glassware including several beer steins and highball glasses. A table right next to the door had seating for six people. They were in Ross' dining room.

Shane heard no sound in the house. He paused after several paces and listened as Ventura came in behind him. There were no voices, no footsteps, and no commotion. He was certain Ross was there, though. As was Dallas. The ghost would not have left them that easily.

The house had an open floor plan. The dining room opened into the kitchen to their right and the living area to the left. There were no walls ahead of them, the area just merged into a pantry with shelves stocked full of canned and bottled items.

The roof was held aloft with support pillars rather than full walls. Many were paneled, wide enough on which to hang art, and featured electrical outlets. Each one was large enough that anyone could have hidden behind it and not be seen.

Shane took a step toward the living area, beyond which walls hid the rest of the house. From the kitchen on the right, he heard the telltale click of a gun being cocked.

He stopped as a man in a plaid shirt and jeans took another step into the dining room. His arm was extended, holding up the barrel of a hunting rifle. He had the butt of the weapon pressed to his shoulder and ready to fire.

"You're trespassing," the man said.

Shane held up his hands and stayed still.

"Is this not my hotel? My mistake," he said.

"Mine too," Ventura added. He pointed his gun at the other man's head. "Federal agent. Going to need you to lower that weapon nice and slow, sir."

The gunman glanced at Ventura, then Shane, and back again.

His arms were steady, but Shane saw the tension and fear behind his eyes. There was also anger. This was not a man ready to surrender.

The man with the rifle twisted his body, bringing the rifle to bear on Ventura. The shot rang out a moment later, the sound enhanced by the tight space. It rang in Shane's ears as he watched the man fall back, his arms going slack and dropping the rifle.

Ventura remained motionless only a moment longer, his arms still extended, and the gun still aimed right where he'd fired it. The moment the dead man hit the floor, he lowered it and approached the body, kicking the rifle aside.

Blood trickled from the wound, just left of center in the man's forehead. Ventura was a good shot, and he didn't flinch under pressure.

"You want that?" The agent nodded to the rifle.

Shane shook his head.

"Too bulky," he replied.

Ventura checked the man's pulse and then stood. Shane spared another glance at the corpse on the floor and then headed out of the room and through the kitchen, tracing the path from which the gunman had appeared.

A hallway off the kitchen led him to a sealed door. The house was still quiet, but Shane heard a faint rumbling from below. He opened it slowly, thankful for the silent hinges, and stared down a flight of stairs to a dimly lit basement.

Shane and Ventura took the stairs into a small basement area. The room was open like those in the house above, but a single doorway led into a darkened passage. Sounds echoed up through the doorway, voices and intermittent banging and thumping.

"How much time do we have?" Shane whispered.

It sounded like Ross was clearing house below. If he had a secret exit and more men helping him, he could clear the ghosts and move through the tunnel system, surfacing God knew where before the FBI set foot in the house.

"Not much if he's leaving now," Ventura said. "Ready?"

Shane grinned and headed through the darkened passage. It was not a natural hallway beyond but a stone tunnel that angled down, a passage into the mines and whatever else lay below the ranch and the valley it sat upon.

The air grew cold and stale the deeper they went, but the sounds grew louder. Shane made out several voices, though he couldn't say whether they were living or dead.

The passage was not long and soon opened into a large cavern that branched in several directions. To their immediate left was a massive metal door fixed into the cave wall with a five-spoke vault handle on the outside. The door was open, and inside was a metal-lined room full of shelves, a desk, a cot, and other items that gave it the appearance of a very small and spartan apartment.

"Fallout shelter," Shane guessed, looking it over. No one was inside, nor were there any of the haunted items for the ghosts that had been caged above ground.

"Looks like it's been here since the fifties," Ventura agreed.

"Except the door," Shane said. "It's from a vault."

He pointed to the inside of it, and the lack of a handle. If anyone was inside when it was sealed, they'd never get out.

Across the hall was another cavern, this one illuminated by a white light. Shane approached it quietly and peered inside from the entrance. The light was mounted on the wall, and the door was less sturdy. The room lacked the bed and living space of the shelter, but it was still lined with shelves. Dozens of them, half-empty now, and the rest dotted with sealed boxes of various sizes. He didn't need to check them to know they were lead-lined, and that their contents were haunted.

"They're hauling this elsewhere. Probably somewhere on the other side of the valley." Shane looked at the empty shelves. Ross and his men were using the tunnels just like Dallas had likely done when he vanished into shadows.

The voices echoed through the cavern, and it was hard to tell which of the tunnels they might have gone down. They'd be back soon enough to get the rest of their stash. Shane didn't care about them, but he didn't want them in the way. He wanted Dallas.

"I'll find Ross," Ventura suggested. "You head toward the mine Bags told us about and look for Dallas."

"Or," a new voice chimed in. "You can both just die in here now."

Shane and Ventura turned to see Ross smiling in the doorway, his gun on Ventura while a man at his side had a gun on Shane.

"Going to need that weapon, Agent Ventura," Ross said. Ventura hesitated a moment, and Shane wondered if he was considering whether he could get both shots off before either of the men returned fire when a third man appeared.

"We've got Feds coming down the main road," the third man said. "I sealed and hid the tunnel entrance again, but they'll find it soon enough. Someone shot Darryl in the kitchen."

The last part was added with a scowl as the man looked at Shane and Ventura. Ross sighed, and Ventura threw his gun to the ground.

"You called for backup? You're on vacation." Ross shook his head.

He approached Ventura and pressed the barrel of his gun into the agent's cheek, staring him in the eye.

"You're a real pain in the ass, you know that?"

"So I've heard," Ventura replied.

Ross took a step back out of the item vault, and into the cavern.

"Come," he ordered, waving with his gun for Shane and Ventura to follow.

They did as they were told, and Ross led them across the cavern back to the fallout shelter they had first inspected.

"Looks like it's your lucky day, fellas. I was just going to shoot you, but I don't want anyone upstairs to hear what we're doing. So, instead, I'm just going to seal you in this vault so you can die slowly. Don't say I never did anything nice for you."

One of the other two men pushed Ventura into the room, and Shane went of his own volition.

"That's it? You're just going to kill us?" Ventura asked.

Ross laughed.

"Of course. You're in the way."

With a gesture from Ross, the door swung shut. Shane watched through the crack as the rancher gave them a smile and a wave before the door clanked into place. The sound of the handle spinning and the locking pins setting in came next. They were locked in with no handle on the inside.

All outside sound was cut off. Ventura banged on the door, but the thick metal ate the sound, even the vibration, making his fists produce the dullest of thuds.

A pair of dim yellow lights set into ancient cages on either side of the door provided the only light in the small room. Above them, a small fan hummed in the vents, and there was nothing else to see or hear. All the shelves in the room were empty; even the mattress had been stripped from the cot.

On the back wall, behind an old map of Nevada, was a second door. Like the entrance, it lacked a handle. Shane and Ventura tried to break it down, but it was as solid as the stone walls.

Ventura searched the room thoroughly, despite there being nothing obvious. He went through the drawers of the small writing desk on the far side of the room and discovered old, blank papers and nothing else.

"Burke will find us," Ventura said after several minutes. "They'll find the entrance to the passage and come down here."

Both had heard Ross' man say that he sealed and hid the entrance to the tunnels, but neither acknowledged it. There was also the possibility that, even if the FBI found the tunnels, the vault door would still be impossible to open. Shane had not paid enough attention to know what kind of locking mechanism it had or how it could be opened.

Ventura did a second search of the room, this time moving the desk in the corner and looking under things as well as inspecting seams in the wall in case there were hidden panels when the light above the door flickered. Both men looked up in silence as it flickered a second time and then went dead.

Shane had thought to make a sarcastic comment but stopped himself as he realized the fan above their head had also whirred to a quiet stop.

"Air stopped," Ventura said, noticing the same.

Shane stood under the vent in the dark and raised his hand. No air was moving. He held his hand there for a minute, waiting to feel any current, no matter how faint. There was nothing.

Although he had no fear of waiting in the dark for a rescue, Shane was concerned about the airflow. If the room they were in had been set up as a proper fallout shelter, that vent was their only air supply. Fallout shelters needed to be airtight with a proper ventilation system to filter if they were going to protect the people within them. That had just been shut off.

"How much air do you think this room has?" Ventura asked.

"It's small," Shane pointed out. "Less than a thousand cubic feet for two grown men. Less than a day, probably."

"That a wild guess?" Ventura asked.

Shane could not see the other man's face in the dark, but he could imagine his expression.

"Just quick math. I could be wrong."

If anything, he might have overestimated. He didn't need to tell Ventura that, though.

CHAPTER 23

THE LABYRINTH

Shane sat on the metal frame of the cot. They would consume less oxygen by not doing anything. As much as it annoyed him, he knew that staying still would keep them alive longer than fighting against an immovable door.

Ventura was restless. Shane heard him moving now and then, though he could not see what the other man was doing.

"They should have been down here by now," Ventura said.

If the FBI was at the house when Ross' man said they were, they were likely already raiding the place. If Ross had left men to fight them, who knows how long it would take. If they had all abandoned it, the FBI might still overlook the passageway into the tunnels. Shane didn't want to point out that they would still likely die before anyone found them.

As if to spite his thoughts, a metallic clank echoed through the room to Shane's right. It did not come from the vault door that had locked them in; it was the smaller rear door of the room.

He got to his feet as a cool breeze filtered in, hitting him in the face.

"What did you do?" Ventura approached in the dark.

"Wasn't me." Shane reached for the door. It was open just a crack, and whatever lay beyond was as dark as the shelter. He stepped out of the room and into a stone passage, using his hands to feel for the wall and guide him.

Ventura followed suit, closing the door behind him.

"I don't want anyone following us if Ross checks on the vault," he explained.

They navigated through the dark. Whoever opened the door had not stayed around, nor could they hear anything ahead of them.

With his arms extended to either side, Shane touched both walls of the tunnel they were in, but after a minute of walking, it widened enough that he had to choose one side or the other.

The minimal light that had been in the tunnels before was gone. Shane wasn't sure if they were just in a section of the tunnels that Ross hadn't outfitted with lights or if Dallas had shut off the power. Whatever the case, it was as dark a place as he had ever been in. Their progress was slow as he had to keep one hand on the wall as a guide.

"Ahead," Shane whispered as he followed a curve in the stone wall.

A source of light in front of them illuminated the entrance to a cave on the other side of the passage. Ventura said nothing but stayed a step behind Shane as he crossed the passage to the other side and approached the lighted cavern.

The room inside was small and had not been fitted with shelves like the others. A ghost stood in the center of the room, the source of the light they had seen from outside. Its exposed bones radiated a soft yellow-white glow. Nearly all its flesh had been stripped away except for bits that looked as though they had melted around the ribs. The barest rags of clothes hung from it. It reminded Shane of the ghost that had saved him in the canyon, only even more degraded.

The ghost had no eyes, no lips, and no internal organs. It was motionless and didn't react when the men entered.

"Hey," Shane said softly, approaching the ghost. "You wouldn't know the way out of here, would you?"

The ghost gave no sign that it heard them.

"Jesus, do you know what kind of radiation exposure it would take to do this?" Ventura said. "This is someone exposed to a detonation. The actual explosion, not someone who died of radiation sickness."

"Yeah," Shane agreed. "I'm guessing something happened in the desert that wasn't supposed to."

"Unless it was supposed to," Ventura said. "Maybe it was a test on live subjects."

Shane said nothing. As gruesome a prospect as it was that someone might have intentionally detonated a nuclear device in range of living people just to see how they died, it also would not have surprised him.

"Can you hear us?" Shane asked the ghost. It shifted its head, not facing him and seemingly not seeing him. Whatever it had been through in life, it had taken a great toll in death. But that didn't mean the ghost was not useful.

Shane placed his hand on the ghost's shoulder and gave it a gentle nudge. It moved easily, shambling forward a step. He nudged again and began to walk, guiding the spirit out of the cave.

"What are you doing?" Ventura asked.

"We could use some light," Shane said. The ghost was an effective lantern. He could help them find their way back to the entrance.

The ghost moved with little prompting and provided enough light to fill the tunnel. They followed the path that led away from the vault and the glowing ghost's cavern until they came to a new cave and a forked path.

"I think that way's north." Ventura chose the path to the right. Shane thought the same, so they followed it, their docile guide leading the way with no sign of protest or reluctance.

The tunnel was winding, and the walls were smooth, beige with veins of gray and black stone. Their footsteps echoed forward and back, and sometimes, a distant thump reverberated through the walls.

The tunnel expanded until they could walk side by side and opened into a new cavern, wider than any they had seen.

"Like bad pennies," a voice whispered from the shadows ahead of them.

Shane gripped the glowing ghost's shoulder to stop it. He recognized Jack Dallas' voice, but they were surrounded by darkness. He could have been anywhere.

"Why don't you step into the light so we can talk, Jack," Shane suggested.

"Light," Dallas replied bitterly. "Can't snuff this one. Clever move, boys."

"Thought so myself." Shane turned in a circle.

"Won't save you though."

Ventura yelped as he was yanked into the shadows on the far side of the lantern ghost. Shane grabbed the glowing ghost and ran after them, but there was no sign of Ventura or Dallas, not even a sound. He ran down the tunnel, dragging the spirit and forcing it to keep pace as it stumbled and wobbled.

"Ventura!" He didn't care if he gave his position away to Ross or the others. His voice echoed back at him.

"Xander!"

There was no return call or sound of a struggle. There were only Shane's footsteps and voice.

"Keep up, Night Light," Shane told the ghost as he dragged it through new tunnels and caverns. It obliged with no resistance, but it didn't help. Within minutes, Shane came to a stop before a new junction, breathing heavily, and listening to the sound of his pulse pounding in his ears.

"You have any ideas where to go?" Shane asked the lantern ghost. It stood still and vaguely moved its head as though it had a mild case of the shakes.

He cursed and took the most northern passage. Something boomed ahead of him, maybe a door closing or something heavy being dropped, but the echo was too hard to pin down. There was no way to tell whether it came from ten yards away or a hundred. Still, he pressed on toward it.

Soon, Shane found himself back in the first cavern they had entered. The fallout shelter door was still sealed to his right, and he left the lantern ghost to approach it, spinning the spoked handle until the pins released in the lock and the door swung open.

The lights were still out inside, but the glow of the ghost showed him that nothing was inside. Ventura had not been taken back.

Everything was gone from the room across the hall where Ross had captured them. All the boxes had been removed, and all the ghosts and their haunted items were cleared out. Ross had taken his stash and left. There was no sign that Ventura's backup had found the tunnels.

The passage ahead was empty and waiting. He could take it back to the ranch house, back to the FBI waiting there, and let them know what he and Ventura had found. But Ventura was still down there somewhere, and the FBI would not let Shane search with them. Nor would they understand what had happened to Ventura or how to look for him.

"Let's go, Night Light." Shane turned back the way he had come. He had sketched a basic map in his head of where he had been so far, avoiding what he recognized and where he knew Ventura would not be.

The maze of tunnels was more than he could keep track of. Every branch led to another crossroads or sometimes a cavern with three or four choices. If each of those led to similar openings, there would have been hundreds of tunnels intersecting under the valley. There was no way to know which he might have gone through already, or which he had never traveled. He needed markers.

Shane plucked a rock from the ground and scratched an arrow at the mouth of every tunnel he entered and an "X" where he exited. He was running into his symbols within 10 minutes, forcing him to choose different paths from the same starting points.

Night Light moved easily, never slowing or going somewhere else. Shane talked to it several more times without acknowledgment from the spirit.

Eventually, he ran across a winding tunnel he had not seen before and followed the curving path in the stone as the smell of something dead filled the space.

The tunnel opened into a new cave. Even in the cold, stale air, the smell of dead bodies was unmistakable. In Night Light's soft glow, Shane saw a handful of corpses. The oldest, in the far corner, looked to be a family. They had to be Jack Dallas' missing victims, each bearing a hole in their partially decayed heads. But they were not the only ones in the room.

Closer to the door, another body that Shane recognized was lying face up, its eyes open and an expression of terror frozen on the bruised and blood-encrusted face. It was the Endless Night cultist Ross had met at the casino buffet. Their business, it seemed, had concluded.

There was no other way out of the cave. Shane heard a faint trickle of water somewhere, like a stream running, but it must have been under the rock. Even with Night Light's help to look in the corners, there were no hidden places or exits. He had to backtrack to the tunnels he had missed the first time.

Time was running out for Ventura.

CHAPTER 24

THE PRICE OF BETRAYAL

Ventura smelled tobacco smoke and sweat coming from the ghost. The stink of the old casino had somehow transcended death and clung to Jack Dallas.

Ventura could not tell where the ghost had taken him. The acoustics were different than they had been in the tunnel. He was in a more open space, probably a decently sized cavern, but it was so dark that he couldn't see his hand in front of his face.

"Don't know why so many of you fools have a death wish," Dallas muttered.

The ghost had hands like ice and steel. They were freezing and impossible to fight against; his grip was unbreakable. He dragged Ventura through the shadows and darkness.

Dallas held Ventura's arms, preventing him from reaching for any weapons. Ventura had an iron baton in one pocket but had not had the chance to use it. Even if he had, he was not sure it would afford him much of a getaway. Dallas navigated the caves with ease. Ventura would probably fumble about for a few yards and be caught again.

"Time was you could trust a man. Trust him with your friends and your business. Not anymore. Everyone wants what's yours. But you won't have it, Mr. Agent. Not what's mine."

"You mean the money you stole?" Ventura asked.

Dallas squeezed him so tightly that it forced the air from his lungs.

"It's my goddamn money! You think you're smart? You think you know anything? They put a hit on me before I even thought about taking that money. I knew they wanted me gone. I took what I was owed. What price would you put on your life?"

"Why did they want you dead?" Ventura wheezed.

The ghost relaxed his grip, still dragging the living man through the dark.

"I was better than them. Everyone in Chicago was fifteen hundred miles away. I was there. People knew me, and they liked me. I was too respected and too powerful. I was a threat to them."

"They thought you'd betray them." The more Ventura kept the ghost talking, the greater the chance Shane or someone else would find them.

"They turned my men against me! Men who were my friends. That was the real betrayal. I didn't owe them anything after that. They owed me, and I took it. That was my goddamn right."

"But they still found you," Ventura pointed out.

"Yeah, well, they were good. I wouldn't have had 'em working for me if they couldn't do their jobs. But they never got the money. That's mine, and it'll always be mine."

"So, you hid it out here in the mines, and they killed you down here for it."

Dallas laughed.

"That's what all the idiots thought." There was genuine humor in his voice. "They didn't kill me out here. I was nowhere near this place."

Ventura furrowed his brow.

"But Bags said she heard them talk about killing you here."

"Bags. The showgirl? Of course, she heard that. Pete and Bava would have said anything to throw people off. They wanted that money, too. They wouldn't have told anyone where they capped me. And everyone knew the Hofstetter Mine was where you dumped bodies and hid guns, booze, whatever. Been using it since the turn of the damn century."

"But you're here," Ventura said.

"Only 'cause of Ross and his goddamn sticky-fingered collectors.

Money ain't here, and it'll be a cold day in hell before him or you or anyone else gets it."

Ventura was losing the plot and didn't understand Dallas' part in Ross' scheme. He knew Ross brought in ghosts from elsewhere, but how had they found Dallas? And why was he running free?

"You told Ryan that you and Ross made a deal for that money," Ventura said, wanting to keep the ghost going. Dallas liked to talk about himself, Ventura just needed to give him a reason to keep going.

"That's what I told Ross. He couldn't cage me like his pets. Was too hot from all that radiation, so he had to dump me. Would have boxed me up forever, but I made him a deal for a year of freedom. One last hurrah for old Jackie Dallas and then he gets the cash. But when he comes to collect on it, he'll be as dead as you."

The ghost shifted his hands and used one to clamp Ventura's mouth shut so they could no longer talk. Doing so freed up Ventura's right arm, though.

Shane's discovery of the radioactive ghosts on the ranch was bigger than either of them had guessed. Dallas' men had killed him somewhere over in the test site, and when Ross' guys went there to collect spirits, they found him with the others. He didn't look as bad as the others because he hadn't died of radiation or exposure to a blast. But his haunted item was still irradiated, so it was underground somewhere with the others, away from the rest of the ghosts where it wouldn't affect them.

The ghost muttered under his breath about people taking his money as he dragged Ventura deeper into the dark maze of tunnels beneath the ranch. As he did so, Ventura used his free hand to reach into the pocket of his pants, moving slowly and carefully to not alert Dallas to what was happening. His fingers felt cold iron, and he gripped the baton.

With a quick pull and slash, Ventura extracted the baton and slammed it into the frozen arms that restrained him. Iron met ghost flesh, and Dallas popped from existence. Ventura fell to the cave floor with a grunt, free but blind, somewhere in the darkness.

Despite being unable to see and not knowing where he was, Ventura got to his feet and ran as fast as he dared, his arms out to feel for anything in his path.

✳ ✳ ✳

Night Light was growing accustomed to Shane's pace and moving a little more easily through the tunnels. It still gave no sign that it understood Shane or knew where they were, but it moved faster and more easily now under Shane's urgings.

Shane had marked several more tunnels with an "X" or an arrow and directed the glowing ghost down one he had not traversed.

He could hear his footsteps echoing ahead of him before the light from the ghost brought a new cavern into view. This one was larger than the others, like a stone cathedral with high ceilings and walls that glistened with tiny bits of crystalline rock and reflected the light.

The new cavern offered three potential exits. The labyrinth and its seemingly endless crisscrossing tunnel system were frustrating Shane. There could only be so many paths he had not tried, and only so many places Dallas could have taken Ventura.

Shane and the ghost were headed into the first tunnel when something pressed against his head from behind, cold and firm.

"Well, look who it is," Ross said, his voice low. "Didn't expect you to get out of that shelter so fast. Where's your agent-friend?"

"Went out for snacks," Shane answered.

"Cute, yeah."

A warm, dirty hand slipped over Shane's mouth, and the gun pressed into his temple on the other side.

"We got a dozen agents in the house upstairs. If you make a noise, the last thing you'll hear is the sound of your brains blowing out of the side of your head."

Shane said nothing as Ross drew him close and held him there. As he settled in to listen, Shane heard faint sounds, muffled voices, and thumps and bangs, the cavern's shape amplifying the noises from above. None of it was clear, but it was enough to let Shane know someone was there.

Ross held Shane, breathing heavily and keeping the gun firm. His finger was on the trigger, and he was alert and rigid. Shane waited for him to do something else. The risk of being shot was too great if he tried anything.

Shane no longer had Night Light in his grasp. The glowing ghost was freestanding, as indifferent and in its own world as ever, except now, it began to move without Shane's guidance. It was slow, and seemed to search for Shane, slowly rotating in place on uneven footing.

Eventually, Night Light managed a half-circle turn until it faced Shane and Ross. It shuffled toward them, its empty eyes focused on Ross and not Shane, even though it appeared to be blind.

"Go," Ross said to the ghost.

Night Light did not listen and continued a slow, simple shuffle forward.

"Screw off," the rancher growled, kicking uselessly at the ghost.

They were face to face, with Night Light next to Shane but facing Ross. Shane watched them from his peripheral vision, unable to fully turn his head because of the gun at his temple.

Night Light raised a glowing, skeletal hand with agonizing slowness. All but one of its fingers were curled under, and that one pointed shakily in Ross' face.

"Jesus Christ, get the hell out of here," Ross demanded through clenched teeth.

Night Light's fleshless mouth fell slack as though the hinge of its jaw had suddenly broken, and sound rose from deep within the ghost's empty chest. It built, second by second, from a hum to a drone to a deep, resonant buzz, and then finally a scream. The sound had an unnatural vibrato, and it grew until it was almost deafening.

Shane winced, and Ross shouted something that was lost in the endless thrum. The walls of the cavern vibrated, and pieces of stone cracked loose, falling to the cavern floor with loud booms.

The gun pulled away from Shane's head and Ross kicked him to the ground before firing pointlessly at Night Light. The ghost kept its finger pointed at Ross' face accusingly, screaming the endless, painful scream that was bringing the cavern down on their heads.

Although the ghost lacked a proper face with which to show expression, and its voice was limited to the sound it was currently producing, Shane recognized hate when he heard it. When he felt it. Night Light was not in the cave by accident, just like all the other ghosts. It had been brought there by Ross to be sold to someone.

Something terrible had happened to the glowing ghost far from the ranch. It had died a horrible death, and the ghost was left behind as a shell of whoever it had once been. Perhaps it could have endured an existence caught in that shell for the rest of eternity if it had been left alone. But Ross had brought it into the darkness and would now suffer the ghost's wrath. Shane was unfortunately going to suffer it as well.

From across the room, Shane watched Ventura stumble in, covering his ears and looking about wildly. He shouted something Shane couldn't hear.

Shane shut out the sound as he got to his feet. Ross was doubled over, covering his ears with his hands. Shane rushed him, hitting him in the face and going for his gun with the other hand, forcing it up and away.

The rancher's nose broke, and blood gushed out of it. The two men struggled with the gun, and Ross pulled the trigger and nearly shot Shane in the top of his head.

Shane slammed Ross' wrist against the wall, knocking the gun free before letting him go to throw another punch, this one hitting the other man's jaw with enough force to break it.

Ross spat blood and cried out something that was swallowed by Night Light's scream. He reached for Shane's neck and Shane pushed him back, bouncing his head off the stone wall and splitting it open. He moved in for a second blow, but Ventura was in the way, cutting him off by dragging Ross to the ground and cuffing his wrists behind him.

He spoke, and Shane could not hear what he said, but he got the gist. Ventura wanted Ross in custody, not dead. Shane could give him that.

More rocks from above crashed onto the ground behind them. Night Light had not stopped screaming. Shane reached for the ghost to shake some sense into it or distract it but pulled away as a fierce, deep cold burned his palm and fingers.

The ghost was impossible to touch now and would not listen.

CHAPTER 25

FOREVER IN DARKNESS

"We have to get out of here before this all comes down," Shane yelled, leaning into Ventura's ear so he could hear.

"How?" the other man asked.

"Follow me." Shane pointed to the symbol he'd drawn on the tunnel exit to mark his way.

Ventura hoisted Ross from the ground and dragged him along as Shane used his Zippo to find the marks and backtrack through the tunnels. They were under the house, so he knew the path to the exit could not be far.

Shane was running point, holding the lighter up while Ventura forced Ross to come with them. A breeze came out of the darkness ahead, and he felt they were coming to another cavern when he slowed his pace. The air was too cold as it came toward him, and too swift for the currents he had felt throughout the tunnels.

"Dallas," Shane said, though he could not see the ghost.

"Bright boy," the ghost replied.

Shane continued forward slowly and cautiously until they came out into a familiar space for the third time. The vault door was still wide open, and the room on the other side was still empty.

Jack Dallas stood in the center of the space, his feet hidden in shadow. Shane held the Zippo high above them and the ghost shook his head. The lights buzzed back to life.

"You'll need both your hands," Dallas said as Shane put the lighter away.

"Get Ross out of here," Shane told Ventura.

The ghost shook his head, pointing at the bleeding man in handcuffs.

"No, no. He goes nowhere. No one goes anywhere," Dallas said, a rock tumbling from the ceiling behind him as if to accentuate his point.

Night Light's endless scream continued unabated, shaking every inch of the caverns and tunnels. Shane had no idea how long the structure would last, but the rumbling was increasing. It was only a matter of time before the valley collapsed on their heads.

"We all need to get out of here," Ventura said.

"Don't think he's going to let us until I make him."

"I'd like to see that," Dallas said.

"You go, I'll follow after this gets sorted," Shane said, looking at the agent but nodding in the ghost's direction.

Ventura handed Shane the iron baton. He dragged Ross to the side of the room, circling Dallas toward the exit.

"I said no," the ghost shouted.

"No one cares." Shane stepped toward him. "You're going to be gone in a minute, anyway."

He came at Dallas from the other side, forcing the ghost to choose which living man to focus on. With a frustrated growl, Dallas turned his back on Ventura and Ross and focused on Shane.

He attacked Shane the same as he had when they first met, forgetting that Shane could fight back. Dallas was used to killing, not fighting, and he was a slow learner. His attempt to grab Shane failed as Shane batted his hand aside and struck him across the face before kicking out one knee. His aim was to get the ghost down and destroy him quickly before the cavern collapsed.

Ventura pushed Ross through the tunnel entrance that led to the basement of the ranch house. He spared Shane a quick look back and then was gone. One less thing for Shane to worry about as he fell upon Dallas, grasping the ghost's head in his hands.

He pushed hard, forcing the ghost to the cave floor while he squeezed, attempting to break the spirit's skull and shatter his head. Dallas cursed and raised a knee, grinding it into Shane's groin and knocking him aside before getting up to stand over him.

"You think I'm gonna let you do me in?" The ghost kicked Shane in the gut. "I'm gonna bury you down here, you bald prick. They're gonna find the lost city of Atlantis before they find you."

Shane kicked the ghost's knee out again, this time snapping the joint.

"You talk too much," Shane told him as he collapsed to the ground.

A slab of stone broke free from the cavern ceiling and fell between them. The light grew brighter as Night Light slowly shambled from the tunnel behind them, entering the space with its accusing finger extended in search of Ross.

The sound vibrated off the walls and made Shane feel like his head might explode. He tried to ignore it, but it was nearly impossible.

His focus had to be on Dallas as he got back to his feet, ignoring the glowing ghost and its devastating cry.

Dallas struggled to get up on the other side of the stone slab, his broken leg crooked and unable to adequately provide balance. Shane could see the ghost's mouth moving and the anger in his expression but could not hear the words he shouted. His lip reading was not perfect, but he understood enough. Dallas was enraged.

Shane circled the fallen stone and attacked the spirit again. Blood flowed from the wounds in Dallas' head, the gunshots that had killed his mortal body. The red liquid was gushing as an effect of the ghost's rage. His face was a mask of blood as it ran down and soaked his ugly, plum-colored suit jacket.

"I'm going to bleed you dry," Dallas screamed, the words barely registering in Shane's ears.

The ghost got to his feet, half-balanced and already falling forward, and then lunged at Shane. He fell flat when Shane stepped aside, landing in the doorway of the fallout shelter. Another slab of stone fell, scraping Shane's right shoulder and slicing him open.

He collapsed next to Dallas, covering his head with his hands while smaller bits of debris rained down. The ghost went for his throat while he was distracted, encircling it with freezing hands and squeezing like a vise.

Shane stood, gripping the ghost's wrists. He then released Dallas' wrists and jammed a thumb into one of the gunshot wounds in the dead man's head.

Dallas screamed, but the sound was almost imperceptible over Night Light's furious roar. He released Shane's throat, grasping for his own head to free himself, and Shane kicked out again, knocking the ghost back inside the fallout shelter and onto his back.

"Night Light! Shut it!" Shane shouted, reaching into his pocket to retrieve Ventura's baton. He hurled the iron rod at the glowing ghost, and it winked from existence, banished back to the cavern where its haunted item was.

"Enjoy your stay," Shane said now that Dallas could hear him. The ghost struggled to get to his feet as Shane grabbed the shelter door and began to close it.

"No!" Dallas shouted. "I was the one who let you out of here! I let you out to kill Ross and end all of this. You owe me!"

"I think we're all out of favors owed, Dallas," Shane said.

The ghost shrieked and scrambled on his hands toward the door as Shane slammed it shut, spinning the handle closed to lock it. Any fallout shelter from when it was built would have been fully lined in lead to protect those inside from radiation. Dallas would never escape on his own.

Deeper in the caves, Night Light's scream continued. The rocks were still crumbling, some loudly, from where he had been sent. The ghost would not stop until it buried everything.

Shane retreated into the tunnel that led back to the ranch house. Another segment of the cavern's ceiling collapsed, and a rush of stone and dirt fell with it. He ran the length of the tunnel as pieces flaked off the walls and ceiling above him. Everything was coming down, and the ranch house would go with it.

The lights ahead of him in the basement flickered as the ground beneath his feet shook. Shane could hear people yelling in the house but paid little attention to what they said.

He ran into the basement and took the stairs to the kitchen two at a time. Something heavy collapsed behind him with a fierce boom that sent a powerful rush of air up the stairs after him, strong enough to knock him flat on his face.

Ross' kitchen was crumbling around him. Glassware fell from shelves, and the walls cracked up to a light fixture in the ceiling, causing it to tumble to the floor on Shane's left.

A pair of agents were in the dining room, where they'd fallen in the crash. They looked back at Shane as he got to his feet and ran toward them, yelling at them to move faster.

The kitchen caved in first and then the dining room. Shane and the agents ran for the front door as half the house was swallowed behind them. The others had assembled outside and were backing away from the house. No one was sure how much would be destroyed or why.

Shane was several yards up the long driveway that led to the gate off the main road before he stopped along with everyone else. The façade of the ranch house still stood, but everything behind it was gone, including the house, the fences, the stables, and all the outbuildings. Everything had collapsed into the tunnels and caves. Night Light was no longer screaming.

Shane left the driveway and sat on the ground, breathing heavily next to a rusted-out old tractor as he leaned back on it and closed his eyes.

"Someone get him a bottle of water," Ventura shouted. Shane opened his eyes and looked at the other man standing over him.

"Cut that one close," the agent said.

"Had plenty of time," Shane replied.

Another agent appeared with a bottle of water and handed it to Shane. He took it but didn't open it.

"Ross?"

"Back of that SUV over there. They caught his guys leaving through a mine entrance. Got a good deal of radioactive items in lead boxes, including human remains. Doubt the dirty bomb charge will stick, but he's got some murders to account for if nothing else."

"So, a lot of holes in the story that will draw attention?" Shane said.

"Not my arrest," Ventura replied. "Agent Burke of the Las Vegas office gets the collar on this one. He can explain it. I'm just here on vacation. I used a Geiger counter for fun in the desert near where they used to set off nuclear weapons and observed an unusual reading."

"Sounds plausible," Shane told him.

"They found evidence of that missing family in the house, and some others we didn't know about. Not sure how much just got swallowed underground, but they can dig it out. Ross is cooked, in any event."

"They're digging it out?" Shane asked.

"As much as they can," Ventura answered. "Why?"

"Dallas is down there in the fallout shelter."

"You left him... not alive, but, you know...?"

"Intact. Mostly," Shane confirmed. "If they open it, he'll be out again."

"They'll find his item first," Ventura assured him. "He told me he wasn't killed here."

Shane opened the water bottle, took a drink, and handed it to Ventura.

"Where, then?"

"Said it was where they used to test the nukes. His killers said he was here as cover because they were still after the money and wanted everyone else to look here. But he's irradiated. They'll search the debris, find it, and seal it for safety. He'll never get out."

They sat in silence for a moment, and Shane looked to the west.

"That's four irradiated ghosts here. At least. They must have found a hell of a stockpile out there in the desert. Dallas was the only one that didn't look like he was burned to a cinder."

"He died after," Ventura pointed out. "Just a coincidence his haunted item was there and absorbed some radiation."

"But the others died from it. Where were they nuking people on American soil?"

The question hung in the air. Shane didn't expect an answer from Ventura because he knew the man wouldn't have one. No one was ever nuked on American soil, that was the official word. That was what everyone knew. The Proving Grounds was just for weapons testing. Weapons testing wasn't done on living people.

"How many ghosts do you think are still out there?" Ventura whispered.

Shane shook his head. He wondered about that, too. How many were left out there in some secret place in the middle of the desert? And why had they died in the first place?

"This could be something big." Ventura's voice dropped even lower. "People don't just get exposed to nuclear weapons and radiation."

"No, I know," Shane said.

The truth was a little more complicated than all of that, of course. Shane knew that off-the-books projects had been run all over the country and abroad. He had dealt with military operations like the Reapers that made use of the dead to conduct missions that might or might not have been sanctioned.

Ventura thought he understood the magnitude of it all, but he was not fully aware yet. Shane knew how big things could get, and how deep some holes could go. The Endless Night had once had access to a nuclear weapon, and he had detonated it inside a mountain to end the cult.

Anything to do with the dead was off the books. If someone had been doing unsanctioned testing, it only *seemed* unsanctioned.

Someone somewhere knew why there were radioactive ghosts in the desert. Someone somewhere had killed people on purpose. Whether to produce ghosts with irradiated items or just for the sake of killing people with nuclear weapons to see what would happen was another question.

"So, what do you want to do?" Ventura asked.

"I want to go back to the hotel and take a shower. Could use some rest; my head is killing me. Then you can get us another one of your sixty-dollar-toast breakfast buffets. After that, I think we need to take a drive and see what's hidden out in the desert."

"Desert's a big place," Ventura pointed out.

"Yeah," Shane agreed, "but we have Ross and his guys in custody. They know where to go."

EPILOGUE

Wind blew in from the south, stirring up dust devils. It was warm and dry, but that was not unusual during the height of the day. The temperature would drop significantly at night. A person could freeze there at night and die from heat stroke during the day. The extremes were hard to get used to for those who were not native to the area or at least acclimated.

People did not go out to this part of the desert. Not living ones, anyway, or not that often. It wasn't just a place no one wanted to be, it was a forbidden place. They had kept people out for years, ostensibly for their safety. It was dangerous, deadly even, but that was not the only reason people were kept away.

The man walking through the desert was aware of the heat but didn't really feel it. He didn't let things like that bother him anymore. He had bigger fish to fry, as they said. There was a lot more to worry about than the scorching sun and lack of water.

The sun had bleached nearly everything around him. Some old street signs had been knocked down years earlier, and they were faded and covered with dust to the point where they looked like natural parts of the landscape. Even the buildings, which had once been vibrantly painted, lively homes, now looked like skeletons of something long forgotten.

The painted homes were props. Everything in Doomtown III was a prop. That was what the sign said in big, black letters. Doomtown III. It was gallows humor, he supposed. Maybe a little darker, given the reality.

Once upon a time, there were yellows and blues and greens and reds. It was made up like a pretty little picture-perfect neighborhood of doll houses. Someone's weird idea of it, anyway. No real neighborhood ever looked like Doomtown, but maybe a bit of old television esthetics and a perverse sense of normal had been behind it all.

No one knew about Doomtown III, not officially, anyway. People who cared knew about I and II. They were even on Wikipedia if someone were so inclined to look. Just part of the program, places constructed to see what happens if you drop a nuclear bomb near a city. That old thing. But there were only supposed to be two.

Doomtown III was off the books, off the maps, and off the plot. As the man walked down the forgotten streets, he saw faces peering out at him from the glassless windows of fake houses. Some had eyes, some did not. Some didn't have faces at all.

The ghosts were not as boisterous as most. He had been to other haunted places where ghosts gathered in abundance. The more spirits, the bolder they got collectively, he had once observed. They fed on each other's energy much like the living did. A crowd of people could fire each other up, make them let loose and get crazy, sometimes for good, but most times not.

Ghosts were not much different in regard to feeding off energy and emotion. Where one angry ghost might stew in bitterness, a dozen angry ghosts would act out. A hundred of them would tear anything living to shreds. Usually, anyway. But not in Doomtown.

In Doomtown, the spirits were reserved, quiet, and docile. They were afraid of something. There was no reason for them to hide in their fake houses, their empty frames made to look like bits of fifties art deco ephemera, and glance out from the shadows like children who heard a noise in the yard on a stormy night.

He had trouble with the falsity of it all. He excelled at seeing the truth. It was his special skill if one were to boil it down to its simplest form, but there was not a lot of truth in Doomtown. The place had been constructed as a lie from the beginning. That made it hard to navigate, in the mental sense.

He chose a building at random, a little house that might have once been sky blue but was now the color of dust and shallow water. No one would mistake it for a real house that real people lived in. The windows had never had glass in the frames. No one had installed a real door.

The house was there to provide a structure, a vague semblance of what people might have taken cover in should a real nuclear disaster have happened. Inside the house was where reality would take place. No one cared about how the walls and the windows stood up to a blast. They wanted to know what would happen to flesh and bone inside those walls.

Ghosts scattered as the man walked through the doorless entrance. At least five of them, though he wasn't paying that much attention. They scattered to the shadows or ducked under the house frame to hide in the crawl space. They fled with the dust devils and the whispering wind to places the living would never see them.

Cupboards lined the walls like in a real kitchen. Inside were shelves covered in dust. One still held a coffee mug. Another had cans of soup and a box of cereal, little bits of the lie meant to complete the image for the benefit of God knew who. Would anyone then or now have cared whether there was a can of tomato soup on the shelf? Did that make the deaths more or less real? More or less palatable?

A once-lemon-colored sofa sat encased in a thick layer of dust on the far wall. A round table in the kitchen was set with four chairs. Each chair held a faceless, featureless mannequin, sitting for its dusty dinner the same as it had been for many decades.

The man paused to stare at the mannequins. He didn't understand why they were there at first, but it occurred to him after a moment. They were props, too. In case someone discovered Doomtown III. In case anyone who wasn't supposed to know about it found out. Then it was just another test site, a place filled with prop houses and prop people. A place where nothing bad happened instead of a place where dozens died. Where flesh was melted away from bone as fast as it took for them to scream their last breath.

He walked up the stairs to the second floor. There was less dust up there but still quite a bit. It covered the once-plush carpets and the neatly made beds. It filled the bathtub and sink, and the prop toilet where someone had left the lid up.

From the bedroom window, he saw distant mountains and a big, blue sky full of fluffy, white clouds. The desert looked enormous and endless from the window. The Las Vegas lights were far away. The fences around the military bases were nowhere to be seen. There was nothing remarkable in any direction. Hell of a place to die.

The man crossed the house to the far bedroom. This one was a room with a smaller bed and a child-sized mannequin tucked under the covers. The dusty, featureless head had a face drawn on it with a marker. Two black dots for eyes and a big, black smile, smiling up at the blank ceiling for seventy years or so.

He headed back downstairs and stood next to the dining room table, looking at all the mannequins before turning to look around the house.

"Hello?" he called out. There was no reply.

The fake house had no basement, and there were no other secret places. It was a basic structure with a basic design. Just a prop. Just a tomb.

There were no bodies in the house, nor were there any outside. The ghosts watched him from the shadows and corners. The bodies were not gone, of course, they were just hidden. He walked between fake houses, past a fake church and a fake bank, to the end of a street. The ground ahead was not flat like everywhere else. There was a barely noticeable surge there.

A hundred people would have walked across the ground and not given it a second thought. There were cracks in the dry earth, but that was true everywhere in the desert. The elevated soil was not so elevated that you would have called it a hill or even a bump.

The thing was, burying a body in certain kinds of substrate causes a risk of gas pockets forming. It's a big issue in cement when the whole structure could crack, but it could also happen in dry, desert soil if it was packed tightly. When it rains, as rare as that is, the earth could form a sort of clay pot, and as the bodies decompose, the gas builds, and the clay cap is pushed up until the gas releases a little bit. Barely noticeable. More noticeable if it's a few dozen bodies.

The man stared at the raised patch of earth. A mass grave, hidden away and forgotten for years and years. Lots of bodies. Lots of links to the past. Lots of ghosts. And there was a hole. Someone had been digging.

He turned back to the town and made his way to the nearest house.

"You." He pointed to a ghost that was trying to remain hidden in the darkest corner.

It thought itself invisible, but the man was not easily fooled. He saw things in shadows better than they saw themselves.

The ghost shrunk in on itself, lowering its head, and pulling into the shadow of the corner, hoping the man would leave it alone. He did not. Instead, he approached slowly and crouched before the wretched thing. It was thin and ghastly, devoid of most of its flesh, and badly burned save for a portion of the left side of its body. He thought it must have hidden partially behind something as it died, something that preserved a scant fragment of who it once was.

"Leave me alone." The ghost refused to look at the man. "Please."

The man knew the dead felt fear. It was a basic emotion, and one that survived beyond the mortal plane. Like anger and hate, it was very much a part of the fabric of many ghosts. But for it to be the chief emotion or initial response was rare. Ghosts only feared when given a reason. Something substantial was needed to trigger it, something more than a stranger's approach.

"Why are you afraid?" the man asked. "What's happened here?"

He could not make sense of it. It was usually easy for him to get the feel for a place. Like finding the bodies hidden underground, it was not difficult to suss out the truth of a mysterious situation when he put his mind to it. But Doomtown had suffered some other kind of catastrophe, and it was playing havoc with his ability to sort reality. The deaths were not the worst part of Doomtown.

"It's not safe anymore, but we can't leave. We can't get away."

"From what?" the man asked.

"I don't know what it is," the ghost answered.

It looked up now, looked the man in the eye, and the fear the man saw there was far more primal than anything he had experienced in a very long time. Despite the melted flesh of the dead face, the one good eye was almost crystal clear. And it was wide with panic, a dread beyond reason. Nothing should have terrified the dead so deeply.

"Then why are you afraid of it? Can you show me where it is?"

The ghost shook its head.

"It comes from below. Deep under the ground. It eats anyone it can find."

The man raised an eyebrow and lifted his head to look around as he produced a cigarette seemingly from nowhere. He placed it between his lips and the ember at the end glowed on its own, though he had not bothered to lift a lighter this time. There were no other ghosts in the house peering through windows. They had all fled. The fear in the air was electric.

"What do you mean it eats anyone it can find?"

"Just what I said," the ghost replied in the softest whisper. "It eats everyone."

Check out these best-selling series from our talented authors:

GHOST STORIES

RON RIPLEY

BERKLEY STREET SERIES
MOVING IN SERIES
HAUNTED COLLECTION SERIES
DEATH HUNTER SERIES

IAN FORTEY

JIGSAW OF SOULS SERIES
CULT OF THE ENDLESS NIGHT SERIES

SUPERNATURAL SUSPENSE

A. I. NASSER

SLAUGHTER SERIES
SIN SERIES

DAVID LONGHORN

NIGHTMARE SERIES
ASYLUM SERIES

SARA CLANCY

THE BELL WITCH SERIES
BANSHEE SERIES

For a complete list of our new releases and best-selling horror books, visit ScareStreet.com or scan the QR code below!

www.ingramcontent.com/pod-product-compliance
Lightning Source LLC
Chambersburg PA
CBHW050345030726
47503CB00008B/2622